THE YOCCI WELL

by

Juana Manuel Gorriti

Translated by
Kathryn Phillips-Miles
with an introduction and annotations by
Simon Deefholts

Obra editada en el marco del "Programa Sur" de Apoyo a las Traducciones del Ministerio de Relaciones Exteriores, Comercio Internacional y Culto de la República Argentina.

Work published within the framework of the "Programa Sur" Translation Support Program of the Ministry of Foreign Affairs, International Trade and Culture of the Argentine Republic.

THE CLAPTON PRESS
LONDON E5

This edition © 2020 Kathryn Phillips-Miles & Simon Deefholts.

Cover design by Ivana Nohel.

Published May 2020 by:

THE CLAPTON PRESS LTD
38 Thistlewaite Road
London E5.

All rights reserved.

No part of this publication may be reproduced in any form or by any means without the written permission of the publishers.

ISBN: 978-1-913693-02-2

ACKNOWLEDGEMENTS

We are indebted to the staff of the Embassy of Argentina in London and the Ministry of Foreign Affairs, International Trade and Culture of the Argentine Republic for their enthusiastic and generous support for this project.

We should also like to thank Ivana Nohel for her ongoing artistic contribution to our publishing house; Sarah Hall for her invaluable editorial advice; and Lic. María Rosario Figueroa at Hotel Legado Mítico for her warm welcome and hospitality during our recent stay in Salta.

CONTENTS

INTRODUCTION		9
I	THE TUMBAYA PASS	21
II	THE BIVOUAC	26
III	A POINT OF HONOUR	31
IV	FEET OF CLAY	39
V	THE ESCAPE	42
VI	GOD'S ETHER	48
VII	THE EXCHANGE	71
VIII	SHADOWS	76
IX	REVELATION	77
X	THE CONSPIRACY	81
XI	THE DEATH BED	86
XII	THE SPY	94
XIII	SELF-DENIAL	100
XIV	THE SACRIFICE	108
XV	DEFEAT	115
XVI	THE VOICE OF CONSCIENCE	118
XVII	GOD'S JUDGEMENT	120
NOTES		123

INTRODUCTION

Juana Manuela Gorriti is one of the major literary figures in nineteenth century Latin America and yet she is scarcely known outside a narrow academic readership. Until the publication of *Dreams and Realities* (2003) – a selection of eight of her early short stories translated by Sergio Waisman[1] – there were no translations available of any of her works into English.

A BRIEF BIOGRAPHY

Juana Manuela was born into a wealthy family in Horcones (Salta) in the north of Argentina in 1818. Her uncle was a priest and rebel soldier who had blessed General Belgrano's flag in 1812 and went on to become Governor of Salta. Her father was also a soldier and politician, representing the Salta province in 1816, when he was a signatory to the declaration of independence at the Congress of Tucumán. He was a Unitarian, who took up arms against the Federalist Facundo Quiroga, as a result of which the family was forced into exile in 1831, moving to Bolivia.

In 1833, at the age of fifteen, Juana Manuela married Manuel Isidro Belzú, a captain in the Bolivian army and ten years her senior. They had two daughters. He left her in 1842 to take up arms against the incumbent president, resulting in his exile to Peru, where she followed. He headed up another revolt in 1848 – this time successful – becoming the fourteenth president of the Bolivian Republic the same year. This time Juana Manuela didn't follow in his tracks, staying in Lima where she set up a primary school and her own literary salon. She also formed a relationship with a local merchant, with whom she had two more children.

Belzú survived an assassination attempt in 1850 but was shot dead in the presidential palace (aptly named the Palacio Quemado) in January 1865. Juana Manuela, who had by this time returned to Bolivia, took command of the forces who remained loyal to Belzú but was defeated in battle by the rebels and had to flee back to Lima. She returned to Argentina in 1874, setting up home in Buenos Aires, oscillating between there and Lima before eventually returning to Salta in 1886. She died on a visit to Buenos Aires in 1892 and was buried in La Recoleta cemetery.

LITERARY OUTPUT

Gorriti first started writing for publication after her husband left her in 1842. Her short novel, *La quena*, was published in instalments in Lima in 1845. This was followed by a raft of other stories, including *El guante negro* (1852), *Una apuesta* (1855), and *La hija de marzorquero* (1858). These early stories were collated into a two-volume collection published in Buenos Aires in 1865 under the title *Sueños y realidades*. The collection comprises 22 stories. Several other anthologies were later published, including *Panoramas de la vida* (1876), *Veladas literarias de Lima* (1876) and *El mundo de los recuerdos* (1886).

El pozo de Yocci appeared in 1869. It was reproduced (as *El pozo del Yocci*) in 1876 in the first volume of *Panoramas de la vida* and later republished by the Imprenta de la Universidad, Buenos Aires, in 1929.

Oasis en la vida, her next novel, published in 1888, is a thinly disguised advertisement for a life insurance company, a reflection of the financial hardship following from a life in exile. In spite of this, she cannot help writing well, and the manner in which the story is told makes it a genuine work of literature.

La tierra natal (1889), her last major work of fiction, relates a physical journey through northern Argentina, to the places where she had lived over the course of her lifetime, as well as a voyage back through her memories of the people and events she had known and experienced along the way. This novel provides an excellent insight into the way of life in Salta province in the second half of the nineteenth century, and the extent to which it had been affected by successive civil and cross-border wars.

No overview of Gorriti's work would be complete without mentioning her final publication (a desperate attempt to raise some money): *La cocina ecléctica* (1890) which, as the title suggests, is a highly personal collection of her favourite local recipes from the north of Argentina, Bolivia and Peru, including a recipe for *empanadas* which is still in use in Salta today!

EL POZO DE YOCCI – HISTORICAL BACKGROUND

Novel, novella or long short story? Call it what you like; one has the sense that Juana Manuela couldn't have cared less.

The action takes place in two parallel periods, the first in 1814, during the War of Independence, which Juana Manuela defines as a noble war, and the second, some twenty years later, during one of the conflicts between Federalists (Conservatives) and Unitarians (Liberals), which blighted the country throughout most of the nineteenth century. The civil wars were overlaid with cross-border spats with Chile, Peru, Bolivia, Uruguay, Paraguay and Brazil. The political scene is too convoluted to explain in detail here, however the simplified timeline provided overleaf gives a flavour of the instability of the period.

As a point of interest, the Yocci well did actually exist. It was one of several artesian wells that supplied the city of Salta with most of its fresh water during the nineteenth century. It was located at the crossroads formed by Calle Juramento, Calle Belgrano, Calle Vicente López and Calle España (which itself was originally called "Calle de Yocsi") although sadly no trace of it any longer exists.[2] The word *yocci*, *yocsi*, or *llocsi* derives from the Quechua word *llókhsi*, meaning "exit".[3]

POLITICAL TIMELINE

1776   Spain creates the Viceroyalty of the Río de la Plata, broadly comprising present-day Argentina, Uruguay, Paraguay and southern Bolivia.

1806   British forces, which had occupied Buenos Aires for 46 days, were successfully repelled by local forces under the leadership of Santiago de Liniers.

1807   Second British attack on Buenos Aires repelled after several days of fighting.

1810   Independence declared on 25th May, as Spain struggled to reverse Napoleon's occupation of the peninsula.

1816   The United Provinces of Río de la Plata – the forerunner of the Republic of Argentina – declares independence at the Congress of Tucumán, under the leadership of General José de San Martín.

1825   The Eastern Province (later to become Uruguay) declares independence from Brazil and allegiance to the United Provinces. Brazil declares war on the United Provinces.

1826   Bernardino Rivadavia, a Unitarian (Liberal) becomes the first president of the United Provinces.

1827   Rivadavia overthrown by Conservatives and replaced by Manuel Dorrego.

1828   Dorrego defeated in a coup d'état by Unitarians under Juan Lavalle and executed. War with Brazil resolved through mediation by the United Kingdom, leading to Treaty of Montevideo, establishing the independent Eastern Republic of Uruguay.

1829 Lavalle defeated by Juan Manuel de Rosas, who is elected as governor of Buenos Aires and is then voted full powers as president of the United Provinces by the Federalist (Conservative) party.

1831 The United Provinces of Río de la Plata is renamed the Argentine Confederation.

1833 Rosas' term of office expires and he goes off to fight in the "Desert Campaign" against the indigenous population in the Pampas, south-west of Buenos Aires.

1834 The *Mazorca* – a secret police force – is set up by Rosas' wife in his absence as the security arm of the *Sociedad Popular Restauradora*, the State intelligence agency. Its primary task is the persecution of any political opposition to the Federalists, especially the Unitarians. Named after its symbol (a corncob), supposedly used as an instrument of torture.

1835 Rosas returns on condition that he is given full powers as dictator.

1836 The Peru-Bolivian Confederation is established as a new state, comprising the Republic of North Peru, the Republic of South Peru and Bolivia. Both Argentina and Chile invade.

1837 The Argentine invasion force is repelled.

1839 The Chilean invasion forces prevail (with help from Peruvian dissidents) and the Confederation is dissolved two years later, with Peru and Bolivia reverting to independent states.

1852 Rosas is defeated by a coalition led by Justo José de Urquiza, the *caudillo* of Entre Ríos, comprising exiled

	Unitarians supported by Brazil and Uruguay. Rosas flees to England, never to return.
1853	Unitarian separatists under Bartolomé Mitre form the State of Buenos Aires and declare independence from the Argentine Confederation.
1859	Urquiza defeats Mitre at the Battle of Cepeda and Buenos Aires is reincorporated into the Argentine Confederation.
1861	Buenos Aires revolts again under Mitre and defeats Urquiza at the Battle of Pavón.
1862	Mitre elected President of the Argentine Confederation.
1865	Start of a five-year war with Paraguay, leading to the expansion of territory in the north.
1868	Domingo Faustino Sarmiento assumes the Presidency.
1874	Sarmiento succeeded by Nicolás Avellaneda.
1879	A new Desert Campaign led by General Julio Argentino Roca expands territory in the South, wiping out much of the indigenous population of Patagonia.
1880	Avellaneda succeeded by Roca. British financiers and merchants begin to establish a significant Anglo-Argentine community. Over the next 50 years intensive immigration from Spain and Italy would more than double the population, from 2 million to 5.5 million.
1886	Roca succeeded by Miguel Juárez.
1890	Juárez succeeded by Carlos Pellegrini.
1892	Pellegrini succeeded by Luis Sáenz Peña.

THE YOCCI WELL

DEDICATION

To María Patrick.

When I wrote these lines and dedicated them to you, María, I could never have imagined that, by the time I published them, the bonds which united us and the sincerity of the most noble of sentiments would have been betrayed, so that this dedication would have to serve as a bloody reproach to you. May God forgive you, María, just as the heart you destroyed so pitilessly has also forgiven you.

I   THE TUMBAYA PASS

Halfway through the year 1814 the South American freedom movement had already been active for five years, fighting battles and winning victories; it was real. The movement had its own armies led by heroic champions, and from the banks of the river Desaguadero[4] up to the citadel of Tucumán our land was rent in two by a huge, smouldering, turbulent and bloody divide, which our parents tirelessly disputed inch by inch against the no less tireless efforts of their oppressors.

In that divorce between a new world, which wanted to experience its coming of age, and an older one that wanted to shackle the new world to its decrepit and outdated order, in that immense unhinging of beliefs and institutions, everything was at stake and all ties were broken; the same disagreements raged within families as on the fields of battle.

At the first sound of the bugle call in May,[5] young men had rushed to sign up with the freedom fighters. Older people, entrenched in their traditions, looked towards Spain; and fearing that they would be contaminated by contact with the rebel soil beneath their feet, they gathered together their valuables and left, disinheriting their insurgent offspring and bequeathing them eternal damnation as their only legacy.

They wandered the land in their hundreds, dragging what was left of their families along with them, following the Royalist armies on their dangerous forays in freezing weather, or leaving for the Iberian Peninsula, abandoning their loved ones among the hostile people of Upper Peru.

Very few of these sad pilgrims would ever lay eyes upon their beautiful homeland again. Scattered like the tribes of Israel, they are now settled all over the world. Even in the most remote regions you will often find, beneath a canopy of grey hair, two dark eyes that stole their fire from the Pampas sun, and a voice with an unforgettable accent will remind you of the shimmering vision of that land, so beloved by God.

However, those who did return were filled with sorrow and melancholy after all they had experienced. They thought that they would rediscover the joys of their youth in their old homes, but all they found was a store of painful memories.

* * * * *

When the sun went down one warm and fragrant October evening, a column comprising a squadron and two battalions reached the León ravine,[6] a magical hanging garden that stretches for nine leagues from the Jujuy plateau to the rocky landscape of El Volcán. This was the rearguard made up of seasoned troops who, after their victory at Vilcapugio,[7] had invaded Argentine territory for a second time and who, being faced with San Martín's makeshift army, retreated, falling back in disarray and shame, having learned a painful lesson.

A lengthy caravan made up of riders, baggage and carriages followed the column, snaking along every single path around the ravine. This was the mass emigration of the Royalists. The rebels' pejorative name for them was "the Goths". They were Spaniards, and they muttered "Judge me, O God" with a bitter taste in their mouths as they left,[8] blinded by wilful ignorance, dragging their daughters along with them, choirs of beautiful virgins, heading straight towards those impious hordes where so many of them would be violated.

Great numbers of patriotic fighters lined the cliffs on either side of the ravine in formation, keeping the enemy under intense and sustained fire. The Royalists roared with anger at the impossibility of returning this deadly farewell from their adversaries who, hidden in the trees covering the mountains, were able to pick them off without fear of reprisal, accompanying their volleys with hearty and prolonged "hurrahs".

Finally, decimated, trampling over the bloodied corpses of their comrades, the Spaniards arrived at the head of the ravine. The hills open up there to the right and the left, forming a vast amphitheatre cut off to the north by the Tumbaya Pass, a deep gully opened up by the red-hot volcanic stream that gave it its name. Imagine a wide gate, closing off the delightful Jujuy valley and opening into a dry, desolate landscape, like the Thebaid desert of ancient Egypt, devoid of all vegetation. Huge clusters of ash-grey rocks tower in disarray over narrow valleys, littered with boulders and briny mosses. Those desert lands swept by the cruel *cierzo* wind[9] and freezing gales were never graced by birdsong; and each of those bare grey rocky outcrops are like letters spelling out the terrible legend, "Abandon hope all ye who enter here".[10]

The Royalist column crossed the sombre pass. It was followed by the huge convoy of emigrants, who turned and gazed sadly back on the beautiful homeland they were leaving behind.

We too, one long mournful day, paused at that deadly gate, and as we gazed upon the valleys brimming with flowers that we were being forced to abandon and at the maze of sombre rocky crags that awaited us on the other side, we thought of death. And afterwards . . . afterwards our joy and good fortune returned, and having lost our

Eden we were content with a blue sky, and we discovered poetry in those crags and we loved them like a second homeland. Is there any kind of terrain, however arid, where the human heart cannot put down roots?[11]

Once through the pass, warriors and pilgrims filed their way along the rough paths into the distance, eventually melding into twilight mist, later to be lost in that hurricane of bullets which for fourteen years would sweep across Latin America from north to south.

II   THE BIVOUAC

Daylight had given way to shadows, the roar of battle to the peaceful calm of night. At the bottom of the ravine, on the left bank of the River León, red flames rose from a line of camp fires beneath the blossoming branches of the peach trees. It was the rebel fighters' encampment.

There were hundreds of men of all different races, cultures and beliefs, fighting on the same side, united by nationalist sentiments, sharing the same life with all its risks and dangers, sitting around the same fire, their various causes united under the same flag, losing themselves in rowdy bivouac discussions, in a whole mixture of different dialects.

There were dandies from Buenos Aires; hard men from the Pampas; fair-haired Córdobans with tanned skin; shy men from the barren lands of Santiago who would eat carob beans and wild honey; and the lyrical Tucumanos, who would hang their hammocks from the branches of lemon trees; people from the foothills of the Andes; people from the blue waters of the River Salado, and the deep-tanned inhabitants of El Bracho, who would ride on the backs of rhea birds, and *gauchos* from the borderlands, who would rip their elegant boots from the shins of horses.

"There's not much food, Sergeant Contreras," said a

mulatto from Salta, addressing a huge man with a bronzed face and wavy hair, as he turned a hunk of meat in the embers of the fire. "Who would have thought that we'd just killed so many Spaniards with their knapsacks brimming with provisions."

"Not to mention those wagons full of fresh supplies. What more could anyone ask?"

"To hell with Commander Heredia and his tactics of sniping from the sides. It would have been another matter if he'd ordered us to charge them from the rear: not one of those Spanish Saracens[12] would have got through the pass and lived to tell the tale. We should all have done the same as Captain Teodoro: disobey orders and attack!"

"Poor Captain Teodoro! So brave, and such a great lad!"

"I would have gone with him myself, if I'd been anywhere near."

"I was on the other side of the river at the time, up in a ceiba tree, loosing off rounds from my rifle at those devils. I saw the Captain charge at the centre of the column, brandishing his sword. *Caramba!* It was a fierce fight, everyone thrusting and stabbing with their swords. Then I heard four shots almost at the same time and it was all over. After that, all I saw was a horse galloping down river, scared out of its wits."

"I was firing my rifle, squatting in the hollow of a tree

trunk, and I saw the poor Captain fall, shot through with bullets. And you know what, I heard a scream that pierced my very heart. It sounded like a woman, but I'm sure it came from him."

"Or it could have come from that Goth officer he killed with his first sword thrust. He was brave as a lion, that Captain Teodoro! And he wasn't even twenty years old."

"Teodoro! Why didn't he have a surname?"

"Who knows!"

"I know. It was because his father was a wealthy and stubborn old Spaniard who said it was a crime to serve in our ranks, and he disinherited him. He even took away his surname."

"So what! Teodoro was a brave soldier—he didn't need a surname. A curse on the man who killed him! All I ask of God is to let me have the consolation of making that man dance on the end of my dagger."

"Where did the Captain fall?"

"Where the river narrows, beyond the five alder trees, close to some weeping willows. Major Peralta's gone to look for his body."

"Hm! Who knows if he'll find it?"

The sun had not yet set and a colony of condors was circling in the sky. Those evil brutes can finish off a man's body in the blink of an eye.

"Who goes there?" a sentry called out in the distance.

"A patriot!"

"Who are you?"

"A soldier."

And a horseman, carrying a corpse in his arms, came into the encampment.

"Over here, Peralta," a man shouted, emerging from the only tent in the camp.

"Did you manage to find him?"

"Yes, Commander," the other man replied, his voice muffled. "Here he is."

The Commander took the corpse in his arms and carried it into the tent, where they laid him out on a scarlet cloak edged with gold, a piece of booty Commander Heredia had taken from the enemy at the start of the campaign.

"This is where passion and recklessness will land a man," the Commander exclaimed, looking sadly at the dead man's bloody face. "Poor Teodoro! It was an act of madness. I know he was only twenty years old but that was no excuse. It was rash and pointless and he's ended up dead! It's as if he did it on purpose!"

"Yes," said the man who had brought in the corpse. "He went looking for it, but it was out of a sense of duty. You mustn't make comparisons between yourself and him, Commander. You think things through calmly and follow your head; he was a man who followed his heart."

"Madmen!" muttered Heredia as he left the tent, which had now become a chapel of rest for the body to lie in repose. "Madmen! If we introduce the bravado of a jousting tournament into this sacred war we'll rob our nation of its best fighters. We'd have a lot more brave men in our ranks if there weren't so many acts of rashness!"

"He was doing his duty!" Peralta repeated. Later, when he was on his own with his friend's corpse, he added, "Just doing your duty. That's all I know about the way you met your tragic end, my noble friend. But you went out in a blaze of glory. Rest in peace!"

And, sitting down on a rock, he buried his face in his hands and sank into a painful introspection as the noise of the camp died down, replaced by the hooting of an owl and the howling of jackals which, not far away, were ripping apart the bloody limbs of the dead.

III A POINT OF HONOUR

A few days prior to the day on which the above events took place, in the middle of a warm and starry spring night, two men on horseback waded across the clear waters of the River Arias, which snakes its way between its two banks scented by an abundance of rose bushes.[13] The beautiful daughters of Salta come to dive and splash around in the backwaters of the river like nymphs in a fable, their long hair trailing in the water's depths.

Absolute silence prevailed, and the only sounds were the buzzing of nocturnal insects and the gentle murmur of the current trickling over the pebbles.

When they reached the other bank the two men climbed up the slope, hid their horses in the scrub and disappeared into the shadows, cautiously following the paths leading to the city which, a short distance ahead, stood out in a vague silhouette against the night's mysterious chiaroscuro backlight.

The heroic city of Salta, temporarily occupied by Royalist troops and surrounded, almost besieged, by Nationalist fighters, if not asleep, was melancholy and silent. Every few minutes, from the depths of the city, came the worried sound of an alarm raised by its sentries, like screams in a nightmare, responded to in the distance by the menacing curses of the Nationalists, whose camp fires blazed on the slopes of the San Bernardo hill on the Castañares heights.

Arriving at the Isasmendi estate, one of the pair of travellers stopped his companion with a tug on his arm. "Here we are. This is the entrance to the city," he said. "Within the next two hours each of us has a mission to complete, in different places. You have your orders from the Commander, I have an affair of the heart to see to. It's one o'clock. Meet me back here at three. We need to separate."

"What? You're not coming with me? I thought that you'd requested leave so you could join me in my arduous task: I need to convince that skinflint Salas to loosen his purse strings so we can buy equipment for our men."

"No. I'm here for another reason. Not a reason acceptable to the Commander and maybe not even to you, my dear Peralta. That's why I kept it secret."

"Affairs of the heart! It has to be some childhood romance! Obviously! You left Salta when you were twelve years old, spent the next seven living on campus at the university of Córdoba, and then you left to join the army. And today's the first time you've come back to the city where you were born. Oh, Teodoro! You're abandoning me for a schoolgirl! I was relying on your eloquence to demolish that tightwad's weaselly arguments. What can I say to that damned moneygrubber to convince him to cough some of it up? He'll give me a big fat 'no'. I can't go back to the Commander with that!"

"Persuading Salas is the easiest thing in the world. Just remind him that we took his son Alberto prisoner at Vilcapugio, and he's now locked up in Callao Prison. That's a powerful argument to mollify his greed."

"You're right. I hadn't even thought of that. That's what I'll do. But, Teodoro, where are you off to?"

"It sounds like you're desperate to know."

"Absolutely. Listen. Beneath these roofs, which look so white in the shadows, there's a few dozen beauties either asleep or lying awake who have captured my heart. Doesn't such an admission make you stop and think that you may have a rival, that you need to reassure the friend who's asking you? Where are you off to?"

"I'm going to my father's house," replied his friend with a wan smile.

"To your father's house? The man who cursed you and shut his doors on you for joining up with the freedom fighters?"

"It may be unjust, but I understand his anger and I won't try to confront him. God in his wisdom will grant each of us the forgiveness we deserve, one of us as an American, the other as a Spaniard. But living in that house, whose doors are locked to me, is a sister who I would like to hug. And there's another space left empty by a death, which I'm keen to mourn before my father, who is determined to emigrate to the Peninsula, takes them both away from me. This key to a side door into the garden, which I took away with me as a keepsake, will let me into that sacred place, where I'll sneak in like a thief in search of treasured memories."

"Forgive me, my dear friend Teodoro! Forgive this incorrigible hothead for uttering my flippant remarks in the same breath as your heartfelt sorrow..."

"Enough chatter. Are you forgetting that time is short?"

"You're right! I'll meet you back here at three."

"If I'm not here, don't wait for me: make your own way back to the camp."

The two men separated and each took a different route, one of them heading straight ahead and disappearing into the winding alleyways of the Banda district, and the other turning to the right, heading for the southern side of the city. Within a few minutes he crossed the Tagarete ditch over a crumbling bridge and entered a street flanked on one side by gothic façades and on the other by high walls, with lush vegetation peeping over the top from those romantic gardens, the inspiration for so much poetry in those venerable houses in Salta.

Covering his face, his sword and the blue uniform of the Nationalists under his travelling cape, the young man slipped through the shadows cast by the walls, with the rapid pace of someone who knows his way, only stopping to take in deep breaths of the night's perfumed scent. A jasmine branch, dangling its white flowers over the street, brushed against the brim of his hat as he passed. This made the young Nationalist look up and gaze sadly at the clusters of trees standing in dark groups on the other side of the wall.

"This is the garden you planted with your own hands, dear mother!" he murmured in a pained voice. "These are the flowers you loved so much. Ah, leave that celestial mansion just for a moment and come and mingle with their delightful aroma. Come and stroke my forehead; it's me, your son who was banished and cursed."

He stopped talking and, pulling to one side the tangled swathes of lianas which covered the garden walls, he felt his way and found a door which he was about to open with the key he had shown his comrade. But just as he placed it in the lock the door opened and he saw the outline of a shadow in the dark void it had left. They both spoke at once.

"What's this? A man leaving Isabel's house at this time of night?"

"What's this? A man trying to enter Isabel's home?"

"Who are you? Do you dare to block my way?" said one of them furiously.

"I'm Isabel's lover. So you see, I have every right to block your way," the other replied nonchalantly.

"Well I'm her brother and I have every right to kill you!" the young Nationalist roared back, leaping on his opponent and making him retreat into the garden.

"*En garde*, you scurrilous violator of my honour," he continued, throwing off his cloak. "Defend yourself, because you'll only leave here in a coffin or over my dead body."

"Go ahead and kill me," the other man replied. "But be aware that I love your sister and I'm going to be her husband, as soon as the demands of war allow me to ask for her hand." And throwing off his cape he thrust out his chest, which was criss-crossed by braiding on an elegant, deep red uniform.

"Ah," said the Nationalist, looking his opponent up and down with eyes full of hate. "You're a Goth! Praise be to God, who has brought me here in time to kill you and prevent this marriage, which would be more shameful than dishonour itself!" And they crossed swords.

The Nationalist wielded his blade in a furious attack; the Royalist used his strictly in self-defence.

"Who goes there?" a voice with a Spanish accent suddenly shouted out. At the same time, the sound of numerous rifle butts could be heard thumping on the other side of the doorway. It was a patrol.

"Isabel's brother, don't run. I'll save you," whispered the Royalist, and he ran through the doorway and closed the door behind him. The young Nationalist let out a roar and flung himself against the door, trying to open it. But it was no use: the Spaniard had double-locked it.

Looking around in desperation, his eyes ablaze with anger, he noticed the branches of the climbing jasmine and jumped up at them. But the moment his feet left the ground two arms wrapped themselves tightly around his knees. He looked down furiously and saw at his feet a white figure, pale and dishevelled, grasping him in an anguished silence.

"How can you claim to love me, you wretched creature," the young man exclaimed. "Let go of me, you dirty Goth-lover. I don't recognise you, except to curse you." And pushing her aside scornfully he grabbed hold of the branches, scaled the wall and jumped down into the street. But it was now deserted: his enemy had disappeared.

Tears of rage ran down the young Nationalist's cheek. "Dirty Spanish Saracen!" he shouted. "I'll hunt you down and take your life, even if you're hiding in the depths of

Hell!" And sombrely, silently, without even a glance at the house he had come in search of with such tender emotions, he strode off into the night.

Shortly afterwards, at the León ravine, witnessed by a thousand heroes, the young Nationalist honoured his vow: he searched out and killed his opponent in the very ranks of the enemy, watched by his sister, whose dishonour he had come to avenge. Surrounded by enemies, he claimed a high price for his life but eventually he fell, shot through with Royalist bullets, at the side of the victims whose lives he had taken.

Peralta collected his body and buried it in the Santa Barbara cemetery, on the banks of the River Chico, amid the perfumed gardens of Jujuy. His grave is covered by a clump of oleander, gracing it with the delightful scent of its pink flowers. The person writing these lines sat there in its shade one day; a day full of painful memories.

IV FEET OF CLAY

Twenty-five years had gone by since those days of sacrifice and glory. The same landscape lay before us; but the drama being played out in it was very different.

Once their noble objective had been achieved, rather than working together and consolidating the freedom they had won, the heroes of independence became side-tracked by fractious arguments and, dragging the younger generation into the consequences of their errors, the homeland they had spilt their blood to liberate was torn apart by fratricidal wars. The old watchwords–union and brotherhood–were divided by their ruinous greed, replaced by mutual hate and mutual extermination. A name, a title or the colour of a flag often made them reach for the knife, as Cain had done, besmirching it remorselessly with blood, darkening the bright dawn of freedom with days of mourning.

Having drained the bitter chalice of ingratitude in large gulps, they did away with the great Bolívar, Sucre, Córdoba, Dorrego, Salaverry, all murdered or executed by their former brothers in arms; La Mar, Arenales and Gorriti had died in exile; and at the time of the events we are about to relate, the champions of Pichincha and Ayacucho, Salta and Tucumán, separated by a double line of fortifications, were busy exchanging death threats, yearning impatiently to lay their hands on their enemies.

What lay behind the conflict between Bolivians and Argentines? A scrap of land which back in the day they had both as one seized from the enemy. Vast, fertile regions were left abandoned to the wild by their owners, while they fought tooth and nail over a corner of barely cultivated land, cut off by the inaccessible foothills of the Andes.

The warring parties were now led by two champions of the sacred war: Felipe Braun and Alejandro Heredia. Braun, a bloody-thirsty murderer, was acting as lieutenant to the Protector of the Peru-Bolivian Confederation[14], and Heredia was acting on behalf of the ferocious dictator of the Argentine Confederation.[15] Each of them conducted the war in the style of the power they served. Heredia would have his prisoners lanced through with a sword, Braun would send them to the Bolivian interior and have them marched to Peru and enrolled in the army. Once across the border into Argentina he tried to ensure that his men behaved with prudence and restraint, as set out in his campaign plan. On the contrary, Heredia positively encouraged the reckless vandalism engaged in by his commanders on the front line who, followed by a handful of their soldiers, would venture off the beaten track under cover of night and defy the enemy's vigilance by crossing over into Bolivian territory in daring raids, as they termed their acts of pillage against people and property, and returning loaded with booty to their camp, where they were greeted with shouts of joy. Such behaviour was celebrated with parties and promotions.

These bold assaults, which involved acts of bloody violence, infuriated the Bolivian army, especially the younger officers who, frustratingly restrained by Braun's icy calm, bitterly envied the wild, audacious freedom allowed to their enemies.

V   THE ESCAPE

One night, at a council of war, exasperated by their forced inaction, the officers rebelled against the restrictions imposed by the Commander on their tremendous courage. A fresh insult inflicted on a venerable old priest had brought their anger to boiling point. The Argentines, on one of their nocturnal incursions, had kidnapped the priest from his own parish church, a few miles away from where the army was stationed, while he was praying for peace and harmony among all men, surrounded by his parishioners. The officers wanted to avenge this insult and the council voted unanimously to demand satisfaction, assailing Braun with a demonstration of their profound discontent.

"What is it you want?" the elderly veteran asked them. "What can I do to oppose the firm decisions of the supreme leader? Just today, I received a despatch from the cabinet with clear instructions on this matter. The Protector wishes to place this war on a proper footing, hoping for a speedy settlement, thus allowing him to concentrate all his forces in Peru in order to rebuff the powerful campaign currently being organised in Chile. How can we achieve that objective if we respond to the enemy's outrageous behaviour with our own outrageous behaviour? You have to agree that in such circumstances, taking reprisals would be unwise, absurd. And, furthermore . . ."

"Ah, General," an officer called out, interrupting him. "That wasn't how you and the very same man whose authority you are now invoking fought a war back then, when you had young blood running through your veins. My God, it's only too clear that patience comes with age!"

"That's the only privilege it brings, Commander Castro," Braun replied, smiling at this youthful outburst with Teutonic calm. "Oh, if only those in the blush of youth could learn how to wait, not only would they have the world at their feet, they would be able to pick it up in their hands."

Just at that moment a sentry called out robustly, "Get back!" and almost at the same time a man panting with exhaustion and covered in dust burst into the tent, pushing past the weapon outstretched to stop him. The man who risked his life to break into this serious council of war was a messenger from the Mayor of La Quiaca, a town ten minutes away from the dividing line between the two republics.[16] He brought news that an enemy force, penetrating into Bolivian territory at various points in scattered groups, had attacked the Governor of Moraya's estate, ransacked it, burned it to the ground and fled, taking as their prisoners the owner and his daughter, the most beautiful young girl in the district.

"Lucía," exclaimed Commander Castro, over and above the uproar of angry shouts that exploded at this news and, with twenty or so young bucks at his heels, they all pressed towards the entrance to the tent in order to run to the field where the army's horses were grazing.

Braun blocked their path. "Stop!" he shouted. "Where are you going? What are you proposing to do? Chase after those bandits? Such madness! Do you even know which path they took in this labyrinth of ravines, where you'll run into an ambush around every bend, where you'll die without glory, without achieving what you set out to do?"

These words made the officers pause. Castro went pale with indignation and went towards the elderly warrior, on his own. "Let me pass!" he exclaimed, in a curt and determined voice. "Let me pass, General, because I have an obligation to pursue those bandits, catch up with them and exterminate them, God willing, or lose my life in the attempt. Do you know who those prisoners are that they're dragging along with them, probably tied to their horses' tails? They're the people I love most in the world: my adoptive father and his daughter, who I recently married, the light of my life. Every minute that passes is a crime for me, an additional danger for them. Let me pass, General!"

"You there," shouted Braun sharply, turning to the guard. "Arrest that man, take him to his tent and place him under guard. And as for you gentlemen," he said, addressing the other rebels, "promise me you will renounce this madness, and reserve your bravery for the many battles we shall have to fight before we have accomplished the great task of building the Peru-Bolivian Confederation."

Forced to surrender, Castro handed over his sword, but not without mumbling the words, "so much the better." His comrades made the promise demanded of them and withdrew with their heads bowed, seemingly resigned.

When Braun was left on his own with his secretary and the messenger, he turned to the former and said, half-laughing, "What do you think about that, then, Mr Diplomat? Wouldn't Talleyrand himself envy me such a tactical stroke?[17] Those lads will still be complaining! But I've put all of them exactly where they wanted to be: with their fingers on their triggers. One of them under guard, from which he'll know how to escape, and the others on a rope that they'll know how to untie. As for me, the instigator of these complicated expedients, although restricted by another man's orders, I still have a role to play: a spectator perhaps, but one who will see the intended result of his own work. What a cunning old devil! Come with me, Mr Secretary. And you," he added, turning to the messenger, "you go and tell the Mayor that by this time tomorrow the Governor of Moraya and his beautiful daughter will be safe in our camp."

"Do you see that bag," said Fernando de Castro suddenly, as he approached the sentry who was on guard together with eight soldiers and an officer who were now sleeping at the entrance to the tent. "Can you see that it's full? Have a look at what's inside."

"Gold!" said the sentry.

"It's yours, if you let me leave here. And do you see this?" he added, showing him a dagger. "I'll stick it through your heart if you raise the alarm or make the slightest movement. Your choice."

The soldier dropped his weapon and stood still.

"Good! Here's your gold. You keep it. Now, give me your hands, because you gave in a bit too easily to be convincing, just like I did earlier." And in a couple of moments he'd tied up the sentry, gagged him and escaped through a hole he'd made in the side of the tent with his dagger.

It was a dark night, but under the faint glow of the stars Fernando could make out a group of men who appeared to waiting in ambush behind a wall.

"Friends or foes," he said to himself, "let's go and find out."

They were his comrades, who welcomed him cheerfully, keeping their voices low.

"And now, Fernando," one of them said, "do you still

think we're stupid, when we interpreted so cleverly the handful of dust you used to blind the General?"

"Oh, now you really are being stupid, Ávila," he said. "How else could you interpret my behaviour? But let's not waste time. Let's go and fetch our horses."

"They're ready, down there at the bottom of the gully. All our finest horses . . ."

"And did you happen to bring my thunderbolt?"

"Can't you hear him?"

Just at that moment a horse whinnied from the depths of the gully the man had pointed to.

"Oh, thank you, my friends! That's what I call having a big heart as well as talent!"

A few moments later Braun, hidden behind a rock together with his secretary, watched as twenty men on horseback disappeared along the winding paths of a ravine, riding like shadows, without making the slightest sound. Fernando and his comrades had wrapped their horses' hooves in canvas to muffle any sound.

VI GOD'S ETHER

The general was standing stock still, gazing into the dark ravine and his secretary heard him murmur, with a couple of sighs, "Youth! Youth! Paradise illuminated by three magical suns: love, faith and hope. May they never leave your sky! Ah, but you are so brief!"

It was nearly twelve and it was a dark night, but the clear blueish light on the mountain tops was beginning to turn white, announcing that the moon would soon be out. On the other side of the ravine a group of riders were descending the steep mountain paths into the fresh Tilcara valley.[18] There were six of them including two Amazonians whose skirts and veils rippled in the breeze. They were riding magnificent horses and had to hold them back to match the pace of four men in their midst, who were carrying a litter. The absolute silence, the shadows cast by the crags and the witching hour of night appeared to be affecting the travellers' spirits, and they proceeded in a thoughtful mood.

The two Amazonians, hand in hand, were also silent. But for two women in company to hold their tongues is a phenomenon like the sighting of a meteor: it cannot last for more than a minute.

"Aura!" said one under her breath.

"Juana!" the other replied in a similar tone.

"What are you thinking about, my dear? I'm sure it must be Aguilar."

"He's never far from my thoughts. But I was actually thinking about how lucky I am to have you here at my side, which in all honesty feels like a dream come true."

"Doesn't it just? Bah! This adventure of mine is like something out of a novel."

"It really is! I can honestly confess that a quarter of an hour ago, as I was walking through the shadows, accompanied only by my two bearers and with my sick mother beside me, I was picturing myself as a wandering princess. And in my fantasy, my mind and body travelled back to those bygone days and I could see us standing at one of those crossroads waiting for an Amadis, a knight in shining armour, to demand a favour from him. But who should appear but a lady dressed in black and riding a charger to match, accompanied by two knights with swords at their waists and crusaders' helmets on their heads. She came up to me, lifted her veil and fell into my arms. It was Juana! Juana, the young and beautiful wife of a general whose army is at war, crossing the front line incognito to reach territory that the enemy might occupy from one moment to the next. Ah, your story has completely overshadowed mine. A poet could turn it into a wonderful epic."

"That's not true!"

"And he'd fall at your feet if I told him everything, if I told him that you braved all those dangers just to go in search of a friend. Where? In the remote wilds of Iruya."[19]

"My heart owes you that and more, my dear Aura. It's a pity I only found you on your way back. I would have dearly loved to have hidden with you in those mysterious ravines. Because the sad truth is that my journey was not only motivated by my affection for you, and if your poet had to tell my full story he'd have to find a place in it for anger."

"Anger? I don't understand."

"And yet you know all my intimate secrets!"

"My God! Are those baseless suspicions still worrying you?"

"Oh, but they are now a matter of absolute certainty."

"Delusions, my beauty."

"Listen and judge for yourself. While I was trying to lay the suspicions you thought were fanciful to rest and rumours about them were running rife all over town, Alejandro himself, the very voice of reason, proved irrefutably that they were true. He announced that he was going to rejoin the army, ordered preparations to be made and in a moment of extreme affection he gave me a farewell hug. That act of tenderness, which had long since been uncustomary, struck me as suspicious. But a woman's heart is always ready to give the benefit of the doubt! 'I'd like to go with you,' I said, seduced by the alluring prospect of travelling to those places forbidden to women, at the side of a man. But Heredia threw this back in my face, with insolence and a lack of affection. He visibly objected to my request, and came up with all sorts of obstacles. But he doubtless saw the look on my face and, feeling guilty, he had to agree, because he was afraid."

"Don't you see that you found him guilty before he'd even committed the crime?"

"Keep listening and you'll see. He very coldly gave me his consent, not to accompany him, but to go and meet up with him a few days later. Don't you understand, Aura? The reason he rejected my company was because he wanted to be with Fausta Belmonte, that loose woman from Santiago who has now abandoned her home, the promenade and the bathing house and all other the places where she used to indulge in her outrageous behaviour. Guessing the whole story and flushed with indignation, I didn't wait for the day Alejandro had indicated in order to start my journey and, accompanied by a small escort, I departed on my beautiful Tenebroso, who has given me greater service than any horse ever gave his owner, and in less than twenty hours he brought me into sight of the camp.

I met an officer on his way to Salta on a mission and the look on his face as he greeted me gave me such a lot to think about that I left my escort in Jujuy and continued the journey alone, covering my face with a mask. I'd already seen the trenches from the top of the hill when, as I made my way along a sunken path I came face to face with Colonel Peralta and an officer who was with him, none other than Heredia's new aide-de-camp, that man over there, Esquivel, from Buenos Aires. Peralta recognised Tenebroso and turned so pale that he gave it all away. Still wearing the mask, I passed by them without saying a word, set my horse to a gallop and very soon came to a high point which looked out over the encampment.

On the vast plain stretching out before me, Alejandro was inspecting the troops, who were carrying out some spectacular manoeuvres. I was hidden behind a rocky outcrop at the top of a cliff and saw the general below surrounded by his chiefs of staff, with a woman dressed in a sumptuous burgundy riding suit with gold embroidery at his side. Guess who it was?"

"Her!"

"Yes, it was her! That shameless woman not only stole my husband, but even the colours which only I have the right to wear! You said I was imagining things. Well, what do say about these imaginings?"

Aura bowed her head.

"Like you, I also bowed my head, ashamed of myself. Crying with rage, I spurred on my horse and made him gallop, without knowing what direction I was taking. It was instinct rather than reasoning that led me to you. Without me realising it, Peralta and Esquivel had caught up with me and were giving me an escort. Oh, how infuriating it is to have witnesses around when one's face is flushed with anger, because of an outrage. Every glance, however benevolent, seems to be cruelly mocking, and the most affectionate words seem to contain the steely edge of scorn."

While Heredia's wife spoke, her companion listened thoughtfully, with her face in her hands.

"Aura, I've upset you by exposing you to the stormy nature of a marital relationship, which you are soon to share. Talk to me. Your voice will scatter the clouds which darken my soul."

"Ah!" the young girl murmured, thoroughly dejected. "I thought that nothing could disturb the radiant serenity of two people, united by God in infinite love and in one sole existence."

"I also cherished that delightful Utopia and I believed in

Alejandro's eternal love. But one day a barrier came down between us like a wall of bronze: the terrible influence of that woman. And then mistrust, hatred and a state of constant alarm slipped into my heart and took up residence there, and I'm bereft of any healthy feelings."

"That's a lie! What about the feelings which bind the two of us?"

Juana lifted the young girl's hand to her lips.

"Now, my darling. Yes, in this cool and peaceful oasis where my soul likes to take refuge from all the tempestuous turbulence ravaging it. Oh, how I would have loved to roam with you, hidden in these remote valleys. I have heard strange tales about them. By what stroke of fate did I meet you on your return? Were you not going in search of that learned old scholar who was supposed to restore your mother to health?"

The young girl went pale.

"He's not a scholar," she said, her voice deeply moved. "He's a mystical spirit who, concealed in an amorphous body, knows the past and can read the future. He lives in a cave, on the edge of a cliff, accompanied only by an eagle which has its nest there. The entrance to this wild retreat is covered by a clump of leafy pepper trees and it can only be reached along a path with some terrifying drops.

When I entered that cave, with my mother leaning on my

shoulder, the scene before my eyes was like a hallucination out of a dream, and I had to feel for my own heartbeat in order to convince myself that it was real. In the centre of the cave, in front of a camp fire burning with dried herbs (a strange, acrid smell) was the figure of a man whose athletic limbs were golden bronze. His long grey hair and his beard of the same colour contrasted with his dark, youthful eyes, which were deep-set and elusive, like those of a bird sheltering in its nest beside him. That torso with its powerful muscles, suddenly truncated as if by a hammer blow, seemed to be hewn out of the reddish rock on which it was seated and resembled the idols found in Indian temples, sculpted into their granite altars. The flames from the camp fire made this fantastic vision so lifelike, that the way his eyelids fluttered and his chest moved up and down as he breathed seemed like a wondrous, intrinsic part of the mysteries of the cave. We stood at the entrance in fearful shock and noticed that in front of the strange being was a heap of leaves of different colours, shapes and sizes, belonging to every tree in the whole of creation, from the *ombú* tree from the Pampas to the *tara* from the high sierra; from the Ecuadorian coconut palm to the pine from the snowy mountain peaks. But these leaves were fresh, recently plucked from the branch. He picked up fistfuls of these leaves at random, took them one by one from his clenched fist and threw them on to the fire, carefully examining the flame they produced and breathing in the perfume they exhaled."

"My God!" said Juana, with her characteristic blend of frivolity and sentimentality. "To think what I've missed! A cave! A monster! The rituals of a mysterious cult! What a way to distract me from my sorrows!"

"Suddenly he looked up and fixed us with his gaze, at once relaxed and penetrating, his eyes shaded by thick white eyebrows. At that moment, with his right hand he plucked out a cypress leaf from the fistful of herbs he was clutching in his left. His face bore an expression of kindness mixed with sorrow. The wrinkles on his forehead disappeared, his gaze melted and his mouth formed into a sad smile. He threw the leaf onto the fire and gestured for us to approach. He made my mother sit on a rock and, as I went down on bended knee before him, seized with foreboding, he turned to me and said, 'I know what you have come to ask of me, beautiful child.' His voice was harmonious and serious, like the sound of a bell. 'I can read your heart. Trust and hope. But be aware that human science cannot make a hair turn white or black, and nor can it return the sap to a tree damaged by lightning.'

'What?' I cried, weeping. 'You who have worked so many marvels will not give my mother back her health? Look at her, there's nothing wrong with her apart from the strange exhaustion which afflicts her more and more each day, for some unknown reason!'

'Your mother will not die from this, but from another illness brought on by this one, which will end up suffocating her. This illness resides in the soul and it's called a mother's sorrow.'

'You're mistaken,' I exclaimed. 'I adore her. I've dedicated my whole life to her, and she's happy to be with me. Isn't that true, mother dear?'

But when I turned towards her she turned pale and fainted into my arms.

'Help!' I cried. 'In the name of God, you're a wise man. Give her life! Can't you see that she's dying?'

'Quite the opposite,' he replied, stretching out his wrinkled, copper-coloured hand towards my mother's head and placing it on her icy forehead, 'quite the opposite. She's at rest now. How many times, in the endless nights, has her insomnia brought on these fainting fits, sinking her spirit into the limbo of oblivion! Trust me: leave her for a few more moments in that lethargy which she will wake from only to suffer. The one good thing I can give her is the ability to invoke and prolong voluntarily this dulling of the senses which for her means happiness.'

As he spoke, he took from his breast a carefully sealed

silver phial. He opened it and told me to smell the perfume it held. But scarcely had I taken the phial in my hands, I smelled an aroma both sweet and penetrating which diffused through the air, pervaded my brain and lent a bluish tinge to all the objects around me. Then I saw them disappear to the farthest limits of the horizon and vanish in a dark fog which slowly spread out, reaching me and enveloping me like a warm, debilitating cloud of vapour. An overwhelming sense of well-being permeated me completely, which seemed to have been swept from the earth, quivering in the steamy waves of a pink, diaphanous ether. Was I asleep? Was I awake? Was I hallucinating?

A cold, faint gust of wind brushed against my face and brought me out of that state of ecstasy. I was standing up in the same posture as when I had received the phial. But the phial was in my mother's hands, and the old man said to her, 'for afflictions of the soul, death or oblivion.'

And he pointed to the phial that my mother was holding to her breast with fervent devotion.

'As for you, young lady,' he added, the brightness of his eyes softening into an expression of pity, 'I shall not say "go in peace", since from this day forward peace will have been vanquished from your soul, but I do say to you "go, and do not return", because the shadows where you wish to cast light hide chasms that will fill your head with vertigo and horror.' And the old Indian, as still as the rock on which he was sitting, followed us with a sad gaze until we had left the cave."

The young girl's tone of voice had become so sad that her companion, despite her acute uneasiness, listened to this fantastic story in the most absolute silence.

"When we pushed back the pepper trees that hid the entrance to the cave," the young girl continued, "and my mother anxiously breathed in the pure mountain air, she sighed as if relieved of a heavy weight and her feet, previously weak and sluggish, walked with a light and sure step on the steep edge of the precipice. Occasionally she would stop to examine the mysterious phial that she carried hidden in her bosom, and a smile of expectation flickered across her lips. In the short space of an hour, that moribund body had been transformed.

But this state of animation, this relief which I had been seeking for her, and would have paid for with my own life, now released a painful sense of unease into my soul, because I realised that it was produced by the anticipation of removing herself for a few hours of oblivion from that unknown martyrdom the old man of the cave had spoken about, and that I had looked for in my own conscience, without finding anything other than love and devotion.

'I shall resolve this,' I said, overcome by the most painful of doubts, which is self-doubt. 'I shall resolve this. And I shall destroy my own heart if there should be any sentiment there that could cause you any harm, mother dear!'

Last night I went to bed fully dressed, and when everything was silent in the deep Iruya valley I got up and, retracing my steps, I went to spy on my mother while she slept. I found her reclining on the cushions of a divan, completely still and apparently in the most peaceful sleep. There was a gentle smile on her lips and in her half-open eyes, and a healthy, rosy glow on her cheeks which had long since been absent. I touched her forehead, which was cool, and put my ear to her breast, which rose in gentle breaths beneath her folded hands, which were clutching the old man of the mountain's phial. How happy she looked, fast asleep in what seemed like ecstasy.

'And yet,' I said to myself bitterly, 'look at your attenuated face, the transparent skin of your hands, your sunken eyes surrounded by blueish circles. What is the mother's sorrow the old man spoke of, that places all the blame on your only daughter's head? Oh, I shall resolve this.' And all alone, walking tentatively through the dark, I headed back to the mountain. I crossed the valley, climbed the rough foothills and skirted the precipice leading to the mysterious old man's cave. When I passed through the group of pepper trees, the powerful wing of a bird brushed against my forehead, eliciting a scream from me which was repeated in the distance by a cavernous voice. It was an echo.

I found the old man motionless, in the same spot in front of the camp fire, but now in the reddish light of the flames he was reading an enormous book covered in strange characters.

'What do you want from me?' he exclaimed, lifting his eyes from the book and fixing them on me with a harsh glare. 'Go now, run back along the path and don't look down into the chasm below.'

'Even if it means my death,' I replied, 'I want to know.'

The old man looked at me with an expression of pity.

'What do you want to know?' he said, his brow furrowed with pained emotion. 'You don't realise that knowledge and pain are synonyms in the book of life. Go away! A few happy days amount to much in the destiny of human beings. Why do you want to shorten them?'

'You said so yourself: from this day forward peace will have been vanquished from my soul for ever. Let it be so! Show me that unknown horizon, where the tempests rage that will envelop my life. I want to see it.'

'Probing! Inquiring! Hungry for knowledge! So be it. Let your morbid desire, that has been the ruin of your race, be fulfilled! Look.'

And, lifting an enormous piece of rock in his hand, he made me lean over the gap that had been left with his other hand: a dark hole in the depths of which a deep puddle of black water glistened in the light of the fire.

'What do you see?' asked a voice that seemed to come from within the cave's sinuous vaults. And I replied, shaking, overcome by an unknown power, 'Nothing, only a ruddy glow shimmering in the shadows.'

'It is a lake of blood that separates the past from the present,' the voice replied. 'Look!'

I heard the screech of an eagle and I felt the breeze from its wings, but the cave was deserted. The old man had disappeared and I heard only a voice that said, 'Hail, queen of the ether! What have you brought me? Ah, yes. Here are the leaves that contain the sap of every region which, together, have the power to evoke the spectre of the future. Look.'

The cave glowed with a light comprising all the colours of the rainbow. A dense, acrid, penetrating smoke filled the space, which separated out into strange clouds. These were illuminated by the fantastic light from the camp fire and suddenly took on the appearance of a landscape. In the murky distance a mountain loomed, covered in vegetation. At the foot of the mountain were the white domes of a city and on its slopes, beside a fresh water spring, was a deep black well."

"My dear," exclaimed Juana, interrupting her companion. "Surely that was Salta and its surroundings you were looking at? The city, the San Bernardo hill and its green slopes and the infamous Yocci well, which our nursemaids used to scare us about with their stories."

"I saw all these things," the young girl continued, "as if through a shimmering vapour exhaled from the mouth of an oven. Suddenly an unknown voice reverberated in the air, but it moved my heart with its familiar, cherished tone. It was silenced by a terrible curse followed by a scream and there at the bottom of the well, which I was leaning over, drawn by a terrible fascination, I saw my own image wearing a bridal veil. But I was pale, inert, my breast torn open by a deep wound. The eagle screeched lugubriously and the breeze from its wings extinguished the fire, and darkness spread throughout the cave.

I was suddenly awoken by a feeling of immense fatigue. I found myself lying back in my bed, my hair damp with dew, my feet battered, my clothes in shreds and still entangled with bramble thorns. The federal rosette had been torn from my corset and its red ribbons hung over my white skirt like two streaks of blood.[20]

What had happened to me that night? Was it a

hallucination? Or was it reality? My mother's voice calling me switched the focus of my concern. What was that sorrow that afflicted her soul, that I had gone to find out from the old man of the mountain, an investigation that had left me in complete darkness and had enveloped my spirit in a chaos of doubts and terrors?

I found my mother with an animated expression, light hearted and full of life. She smiled sweetly, but when I went to ask her the meaning of the Indian's mysterious words, she sealed my lips with a kiss and told me to make arrangements for our immediate return, because news had come in the night of the approach of a Bolivian force that had been summoned by the leaders of a plot that was being organised in Iruya.

That morning, when we left the valley, following the wrong path, in the distance I glimpsed the cliff and the clump of pepper trees covering the mouth of the cave. Up in the canopy of those trees there was a motionless black form. It was the eagle from the cave which before long took to the wing, swooping over our heads in huge circles, emitting hoarse screeches that echoed across the mountains."

"That really is a story, a marvellous story," Juana exclaimed. "My God! To think what I've missed! Why did I get here so late? I wouldn't have gone to ask that wise man the secret of the future, I'd have asked him for the power to punish: a quiverful of lightning bolts at my command!"

"My dear, there's no point trying to joke about it. Your hands are cold and clammy."

"That's because I'm angry. Oh, one day I'll go in search of that man and if I ask him to reveal anything, it will be how to put an end to perfidy, to the betrayal of oaths made at the foot of the altar!"

"Aren't you tempted to follow the example of the women's chatter?" Colonel Peralta suddenly said to his young companion.

"Oh yes, Colonel, but you seemed so deep in your thoughts!"

"Just distant memories of these parts, from another time when I came through here in pursuit of the enemy."

"We'll soon be back here, doing exactly the same."

"Oh no, not exactly the same. That was a holy war; this a fratricidal one. What do either of the two have in common?"

"That's true, Colonel. I didn't mean to make a comparison with those glorious times. I respect them and venerate them too much to profane their illustrious memory with frivolous remarks. Let's change the subject. So, who is this striking young lady? I can't see her face in the dark, but it must be divine if her enchanting figure is anything to go by."

"She's an exotic flower, transplanted to our soil by one of those dazzling fugitives who abandoned her to follow the Royalist flag," replied Peralta, whose favourite topic was the history of that period. "The girl's father was a senior officer in the Royalist army who died in Ayacucho. He was a nobleman, whose title has an interesting history. King Fernando VII, who was much given to games of strength, excelled at lifting weights, and no one could be found to equal him throughout all his kingdoms. One day a messenger came and told him that on the outskirts of Pamplona there was a shepherd who was so strong that he had defeated not only all the competitors in the region, but everyone who had come from far and wide to challenge him, attracted by his fame.

"Bring him to me!" Fernando exclaimed, and messengers departed within the hour in search of the shepherd, who was brought to the court and presented to the King. He was a young man with a handsome face, good-looking, well-built and self-confident, who crossed the castle courtyard assuredly as if it were the entrance to his cottage, and he looked the King in the eye as though they were equals.

Placed in the royal arena, he laughed at his august rival's formal manners and once the competition started, the weights on the shepherd's bar left the monarch trailing far behind. As soon as he was declared the winner, he put on his shepherd's bag and picked up his crook. The loser snatched it from his hands.

"You have measured up to your King," he said, "so you can no longer be a commoner. I name you Count of the Bar, a nobleman and a knight. Cousin," he continued, turning to the Duke of Alba, "bring him the golden spur." The shepherd knew how to play the role of Count to perfection and no Bourbon was prouder of his coat of arms and sword since the days of Enrique IV. He came to America as a high-ranking officer in the Spanish army, and he chose as his Countess a beautiful girl born in Salta to a stubborn Royalist, who had dragged his family along with him following Pezuela's troops, trampling over the body of his own son.[21] Because in that nest of Royalists there had grown a patriotic hero, by the name of Teodoro . . ."

Peralta's young companion took advantage of the emotion which choked off the older man's voice, and said, "Well, I think the shepherd's daughter is worthy not only of the bars on her coat of arms, but Isabel's throne as well, on account of her elegant poise and the consummate skill with which she handles that lively horse."

"Slow down, my friend! Don't waste your powder on firing rounds to celebrate another man's triumph."

"And who would that fortunate mortal be?"

"Colonel Aguilar, the man of the moment, the general's favourite, the hero who wears a Gaucho outfit."

"To be fair, Colonel, you should add 'the bravest of all the brave sons of Corrientes'. If only I could fall in love with this young lady, so I could have such a noble rival."

At that moment the moon crept over the mountaintop and illuminated the countryside and the caravan of riders.

"Ah," the officer exclaimed. "This sweet Aura was the most beautiful girl in Salta, the same Aurelia who dazzled us at the dance that the General's wife arranged to celebrate our arrival along with the Tucumán division. I only saw her for a moment, because at midnight I left for Jujuy on a mission. It was precisely at that moment that she was dancing with Aguilar, and all the other dancers stopped to watch the beautiful couple, he in his Gaucho outfit and she dressed in pink and white muslin, wearing a garland of flowers and her curly blond hair flowing in waves like a golden cloud."

"Note the contrast now between that beauty with blond hair and blue eyes and the dark, passionate, expressive beauty of the general's wife."

"She has eyes like flames and black ringlets which could have been curled by the African sun."

"She's so vivacious! And light and lithe, arousing passion that a panther would envy."

"For example, this afternoon . . ."

"Be quiet!"

"Our mistress is so pale!" said one of the bearers to the other, nodding towards the litter, its curtains flapping open in the breeze and allowing them to see an emaciated face, deathly pale but whose fine features and faultless rectitude had retained the traces of a great beauty. Her pale forehead with its sunken temples reclined with abandon on a soft feather cushion, frowning from time to time as if she were gripped by a painful dream. Resting on the cushion beside her cheek, a hand as white and transparent as wax clutched in its fingers a silver phial.

"Ah!" said the servant in pained tones, "however much one tries to ignore it, out of affection, the truth is plain enough to see in her eyes: her heart is well and truly broken."

"This all dates back to a long ago," the other servant said, shaking his head sadly. "Since she saw her brother killed, the mistress hasn't been happy for one single day, for all that good fortune has showered her with material goods. She was rich and married to a wealthy nobleman who adored her, and she travelled the sumptuous regions of Peru from end to end, but she was always sad. And she visited all those cities of magical fame: Chuquisaca, Potosí, Cuzco and Lima like a lost soul, looking without seeing.

When her little girl was born she scarcely found a flicker of joy and even then, while she held her to her breast, I saw her weep, looking away from the innocent creature, as if it pained her to feed her."

Then the caravan, emerging from a narrow gully they had been following for a while, suddenly opened out into the Tilcara valley. "This is the place where we tore apart the Spanish troops," Peralta suddenly shouted out, gripped with enthusiasm, and he pointed to the rocky dry river bed in a bend in the Valley. "It was down there that we charged them so violently that not one of them escaped, and before they knew it we were upon them and our lances had them pinned against the rocks."

A sad moan was the only reply. "Mother," the young blonde girl exclaimed and, drawing up her horse, she leaned over the litter. "Try to sleep," she said, after she had stroked the invalid's forehead. "Although, however deeply she sleeps, she can hear everything that's said around her, and if it's something that upsets her she weeps and sighs, as she's doing now."

"A curse on idle tongues and their ancient stories!" said the vivacious dark-haired lady, with mock irritation. "Let us hope God does not allow those poor Spaniards to appear suddenly, armed to the teeth, to settle accounts for their perforated hides!"

VII   THE EXCHANGE

At that very moment, as if summoned up by Juana's words, twenty riders on decent mounts and armed with pistols and swords suddenly emerged from the hollow that Peralta had pointed out and (exactly as had happened to the Spanish troops) before he and his companion realised it they had been surrounded, disarmed, and had their arms bound behind their backs and tied to their own horses, despite their fury.

Juana advanced resolutely towards the commander of the mysterious squadron.

"What right have you to lay your hands on free men who are going about their business?"

"Do you think the right of reprisal counts for nothing?" he replied, in a voice that made Aurelia tremble, although she could not remember where she had heard it before, and by a strange coincidence, there in the depths of the litter a kind of deep-seated emotion made the moribund body of the invalid shudder, and a weak cry issued from her chest and her closed eyelids fluttered.

"I deeply regret," the Commander continued, "having to speak discourteously and even severely to those for whom my respect is a true religion."

"Cowards," shouted Peralta and his companion at the

same time, as they struggled to break their bonds.

"A gag for those men," the Commander said, turning to his followers. "And as for the ladies, I request them to follow us without trying to resist."

"My God! And what about my mother," Aurelia shouted, jumping down from her horse and running to stand in front of the invalid.

The Commander was moved, in spite of himself. He dismounted and approached the young woman. Then they looked at each other for the first time. Only God knows the mystery of such instant attractions, an insuperable allure that grips the soul in the turn of a phrase or a look, obliging both the young lady and the stranger to place a hand on their hearts to question it.

"Commander Castro!" shouted one of his men. "There's a column of men up there," he said, pointing to a cliff that ascended steeply from the river bed. Indeed, marching along the edge of the cliff was a detachment of men, their assorted weapons glittering in the moonlight. At their centre was an unarmed man with his head bowed, followed by a woman wearing a white dress, with long hair flowing down from her bare head.

"It's them," the Commander exclaimed. "Lucía and her father. Comrades, I need ten men to stay here to guard the prisoners and the rest of you come with me, up this slope."

"Who goes there?" shouted a loud voice from the top, making Aurelia shout with joy.

"Bolivia and her men, on the look-out for warmongers," Commander Castro replied. At the sound of his voice, the woman in white tried to jump off the cliff, but the man behind her stopped her.

"Fire!" shouted the voice who had asked 'who goes there?'

"Stop in the name of heaven," Aurelia exclaimed. "I'm being held prisoner with my mother and . . ."

"And General Heredia's wife," said Juana, finishing the sentence. "Dear Aguilar, don't add an ounce of lead to our painful misadventure."

When Juana said these words, there was a noise like a mountaintop collapsing and out from a cloud of dust there fell (rather than appeared) a rider brandishing a sword, mounted on a lively steed, dressed in a flamboyant outfit, handsome, majestic and terrible. Looking all around with gleaming eyes, he thrust himself into the centre of the group, which bristled with unsheathed swords menacing him, in an attempt to reach the spot where the prisoners were being held.

Castro went up to face him. "Nobody touch that man," he said, turning to his companions. "He's mine."

"Oh, so you're the commander of these kidnappers?" the

man asked.

"Oh, so you're the commander of those bandits?" the other responded, and they crossed swords. Aurelia threw herself between them and separated them.

"What are you going to do," she exclaimed. "Kill each other? This is madness. If you kill Aguilar," she said, turning her gentle gaze upon Castro, "that will be the death sentence of the people you've come to rescue. And if you were to kill the commander of the force that has us in their power, it goes without saying that you'd be next, Aguilar. You're not afraid of death, but would you want to leave me all alone in this world, when as you know a rosy future lies ahead of us together?"

Aguilar, subdued by these seductive images, lowered his sword, and replied in a tender voice in stark contrast to his bellicose stance, "Whatever you say, my sweetheart. What must I do?"

Aurelia turned to Castro, a pleading look in her eyes. The young man sighed and also lowered his sword, murmuring in a voice so low that only Aurelia's heart could hear him, "Whatever you desire, angel from heaven. You shall have your wish!"

"Thank you, brave gentlemen," the young lady exclaimed, stretching out her arms towards both of them so affectionately that something like a shadow flashed across Aguilar's dark eyes.

"Well then!" the young lady continued. "The laws of combat allow prisoners the hope of freedom by means of an exchange. So, exchange us for your prisoners and we shall go our separate ways as friends, and all content."

A few moments later the two detachments came together and, after making the exchange, one group ascended the Oquia hill while the others went down along the valley floor to take the low road to Ornillos, not before Commander Castro's dark eyes had turned frequently to seek out a pair of blue ones that flashed him a smile. For that reason, no doubt, the beautiful daughter of the Governor of Moraya lowered her own eyes, never to look up again.

VIII SHADOWS

When the two enemy parties had lost sight of each other, Aurelia felt a painful emotion, something indefinable, unknown, which filled her heart with a strange doubt. She looked at Aguilar and saw that he looked sombre. She turned to Juana, who looked at her with an expression that made her even more perplexed. She took refuge next to her mother and found her awake, sitting up but very pale and staring intently back the way they'd come with her large eyes full of anxiety.

IX   REVELATION

General Braun had kept the promise he had made to the Mayor of La Quiaca. The Governor of Moraya and his beautiful daughter, escorted by their daring liberators, entered the Bolivian camp the following day.

Disciplinary rigour dictated that the General should punish the misdemeanour that he himself had so astutely incited. He therefore arrested the guilty parties and put them on trial, but the Governor and his daughter pleaded for their freedom with such pressing requests that they gave him the priceless opportunity to put the finishing touches to his work and pardon the crime in recognition of the result.

Lucía left with her father that afternoon, and he requested Fernando to accompany them to Moraya. The young man had not had the chance to speak in private to his fiancée: she had carefully avoided it. To the others, her voice and facial expression always showed the sweet affection fitting for the man who was to be husband. No one had noticed the slightest change in her: no one except Fernando. The young man couldn't understand why his heart felt as it did. He was out of sorts with himself and he was keen to reach their destination, hoping to find, in that house where he had spent his childhood, where his love for

Lucía had first flourished, memories of a past that was fading despite his best efforts. But the house, which had previously seemed to him like a lover's paradise, now felt as cold as a burnt out fire. A star that had risen in its firmament, which had been eclipsed before it had a chance to shine.

The Governor, entering the room followed by his daughter, came to interrupt his painful reverie.

"Fernando," he said. "The time has come to make a revelation that will have an enormous impact on your life and which I've held back until today, for reasons I'll explain and that I know you'll find justified. I wanted Lucía to be here too, because it's going to change both of your destinies."

He sat down opposite the young man and made his daughter sit beside him. Then he continued. "All you know about your past history is the painful scene that night when a woman in mourning, wearing a veil and carrying a new-born babe in her arms, knocked on the door of a poor labourer in Jalina and, throwing herself at his feet, begged him to provide shelter for a poor child who had come into this world semi-orphaned and shrouded in dishonour. She left there sobbing and desperate, returning every day late at night to hug her son and weep, until one day she disappeared, never to return."

"Yes," Fernando replied, deeply moved. "I was that child, and you were that labourer, dear father, and you surrounded me with care and affection, found yourself a wife to provide me with a mother, showed me how to love work, taught me about the horrors of vice and the excellence of virtue, and as if those were not benefits enough from your kindness, you're going to give me this beautiful and noble companion."

Lucía's eyes and lips sent the young man a sweet and pallid smile.

"All these things, my son," the old man replied, "filled my heart with an immense joy. But what you don't know is that, each and every day since your mother placed you in my arms, I have deprived you of something very substantial. Do you know what? I've left you in ignorance of the fact that you are a rich man.

From a very early age I noticed that you had the soul of a dreamer who liked to live in an idealised world. To encourage this propensity would have been to open the door to idleness. So I kept quiet about the treasure your mother entrusted me to keep for you. I took upon my shoulders the heavy burden of responsibility for your future and I devoted myself to looking after your interests. All the wealth that you've seen me accumulate so greedily was yours, it was for you. I have here an up-to-date statement of your fortune," the old man continued, placing a weighty tome on the table that Fernando was leaning on. "The Governor of Moraya's immense wealth, his proverbial wealth, is yours, and yours alone."

"It belongs to Lucía, father," Fernando exclaimed, holding out his arms to the old man. "I already have a treasure: this sword of mine which, I hope, will open up a broad path for me in the world."

"And since I am about to leave the world, I need nothing, desire nothing, want nothing apart from peace and oblivion," the young girl replied. And holding out a cold hand to Fernando she added, in a sad but assured tone, "Farewell, my brother. A chasm will soon separate us, but there in the sanctuary where I'm going to seek refuge from life's sorrows, I shall always think of you, and my soul will never abandon you." And to the astonishment of both the young man and the old man Lucía pressed her pale lips on the forehead of one and the hand of the other, and left the room. Two days later Lucía departed for Chuquisaca to take the veil in the Carmelite convent.

X THE CONSPIRACY

"Castro, the knight of daring adventures," Braun said one day to Commander Castro. "Have I got a mission for you!"

"Don't hesitate when it comes to that type of order, General," Fernando replied, his heart beating hard.

"Read this despatch that I received today."

"The malcontents are calling out to us. And they're hatching a conspiracy in Salta! What a stroke of luck! What are my orders, General?"

"Go there incognito and come to an agreement with the two leaders so that, on the day indicated, you lead from the front, heading up the movement."

"May it please God, General, let me have your orders to set off right now."

"Hm! Commander Castro! Commander Castro! Either I'm much mistaken, or you're thinking about those ladies you took prisoner and their pretty eyes . . . Anyway, you look so happy that, I agree, you do need to leave straight away."

Leave! Arrive! Search for her! Find her! Can my heart cope with this huge wave of happiness?

Let us return once more to that white city at the foot of the San Bernardo hill, bathed in perfumed fronds. Twenty-four years have gone by and it is the same as ever, with its magnificent ancient houses, surrounded by gardens, their courtyards shaded with vines loaded down with grapes and their Moorish roof gardens etched into the blue sky. The night stretches its veil over the city, sprinkled with stars, giving it a fantastic quality, but its peaceful calm has been broken by the clamour of arms and the warlike sound of bugles.

Fresh reinforcements sent by Rosas to the army of the North had entered Salta that afternoon and Heredia, together with Aguilar and another two of his bravest commanders, reliably informed of a conspiracy being plotted in the city with the connivance of Braun and also involving the newly arrived troops themselves, had left their encampment and gone to receive them, in the hope of uncovering and putting down the conspiracy in time.

Slipping past under cover of darkness and the crowds, a man who had just set foot in a derelict house where it seemed he had been expected, his face hidden between the lapel of his cape and the brim of his hat, crossed the school bridge, descended the Calle de Cebrián and stopped at the corner of the square.

"La Merced barracks," he said, consulting a piece of paper on which, doubtless, were written directions to certain points in the unfamiliar city. "At nine o'clock our people will relieve the guard. San Bernardo barracks," he continued, "Still nothing done with this group which is closely watched by Aguilar, its colonel . . ." The undercover officer suppressed a sigh which was more like a muted curse, and continued. "Our agent has undertaken to buy off the non-commissioned officers and take the barracks at eleven o'clock tonight. It's seven o'clock. Two hours," he added in a voice in which the most intimate chords of his heart seemed to resonate. "Two hours to find a way to see her and immerse my soul in a world of happiness for that short space of time. Let's go!"

He crossed the southern fringes of the city, following the length of the same street along which another man had once, like him, come searching furtively in the night. But instead of stopping by the little gate hidden by vegetation, through which the earlier warrior had entered, the undercover officer turned the corner of the street and entered through another gate, with tall buildings either side, and found himself in front of the façade of a house that looked centuries old, but which was graced throughout by fine architecture. The undercover man paused before the strange spectacle before his eyes.

In the courtyard of that house, two lines of men in ceremonial attire were carrying large candles, and through the open doors of the lavishly lit reception rooms came the occasional sound of bells ringing in the chapel within. A cold sweat ran across the undercover officer's scalp. He found a path through the crowd and, mingling, made his way into the inner rooms of the sumptuous residence. A moan of pain and rage escaped his chest.

What did he see?

Kneeling at the foot of a bed, in which a moribund woman was lying, were General Heredia and his wife, and between them in the same pose were Colonel Aguilar and the beautiful Aurelia, who had been called the beauty of Salta by the enthusiastic young officer from Buenos Aires. Her blue eyes were bathed in tears and, dressed all in white and wearing a long veil over her curly blond hair, she looked like a heavenly vision.

At the head of the bed, at an altar covered in flowers, a priest was preparing the holy unction in order to anoint the sick woman, who seemed to be immersed in deep thought, her eyes fixed on the young woman. At the back of the room, the servants of house were lying prostrate, weeping and praying.

"Ah," said one of the servants, who was next to him, "what a moment to bless a marriage!" The mistress of the house had delayed it until now, doubtless because of the strong repugnance she always felt for this Colonel Aguilar, whom her daughter worshipped, but the fear of leaving her all alone in the world was more powerful than her aversion.

"If you ask me, our mistress was right. On the surface he seems like he's a good fellow, but there's something about him . . . And you know what they say, an officer who's cruel to his soldiers must be a bad apple. But these young girls see everything through rose-coloured spectacles!"

Once he had finished the lugubrious rite of extreme unction, the priest picked up a garland of lilies and placed it on the bride's blond hair. Taking her hand and putting it in Aguilar's, he asked the solemn questions and bound them together for ever.

XI THE DEATH BED

The priest's words were met with a muted curse. Aurelia heard it and a strange vision of the cave of Iruya flashed through her mind. Terrified, she gave a furtive glance around her and her eyes met with those of the stranger.

At that moment there was a rumble of voices and clanking of weapons in the adjacent room and at the same time Colonel Peralta suddenly burst into the middle of the room, followed by a handful of soldiers. "This man is Braun's agent," he shouted, pointing to the stranger. "This man is the leader of the plot which was to have broken out tonight. Seize him!"

Heredia and Aguilar unsheathed their swords, but the stranger, throwing aside his cape, also revealed his and, quick as a flash, brandished it in all directions, wounding Peralta, barging his way through the crowd and rushing outside. Aguilar gave his wife a sombre look and went after the fugitive.

Seeing the stranger surrounded by his enemies and threatened with death, Aurelia was ready to jump in front of him to protect him, but a glance at her mother's bed stopped her in her tracks. The dying woman was sitting bolt upright, almost standing, with her eyes glued on the stranger and with her arms outstretched towards him, struggling in vain to say something that her frozen tongue could not articulate. And when she saw him disappear behind the gleaming swords held at his chest, she emitted a dull groan and tumbled into her daughter's arms, at the same time as Esquivel, Heredia's young aide-de-camp, came in bringing the General the news that Fernando de Castro, Braun's agent and the leader of the conspiracy that had just been suppressed, had been arrested. A glimmer of cruel delight flashed across Heredia's eyes, and the next day this was manifested in a whole host of cruel tortures.

In the meantime, he ordered that the prisoner be put in chains and locked up in one of the dungeons at the San Bernardo barracks, while a court martial was assembled to try him. And, with a sinister smile as he gave that order, he offered his wife his arm and retired from the room. Juana wanted to stay with Aurelia, but her friend asked her to leave her alone with her mother. She said goodbye with a tender hug and went to sit at the head of the bed. The dying woman took her daughter's hands between her own, which were cold and damp, and signalled for something to write with. She had lost the power of speech. Aurelia, drenched in tears, obeyed her.

The sick woman pulled her daughter's head towards her, placed her lips–already paralysed by the proximity of death–on her forehead and signalled that she should go and fetch the priest. Aurelia reluctantly surrendered her position to God's minister, and went and shut herself away in her room. Kneeling beside the nuptial bed, which was empty and sinister as a coffin, the young woman rested her head (still garlanded with flowers but cold and pale) on the pillow and sank into a painful trance.

The sound of a bell ringing pulled her brusquely out of that strange state, somewhere between delirium and prayer. She rose to her feet eagerly and ran to the sick woman's room. But as she crossed the threshold she gave a shout and fell to her knees. Her mother lay motionless on the bed where moments before she had said goodbye to her with a caress, her face hidden in the folds of a shroud.

The priest stood at the head of the death bed with one hand pointing up to heaven; with the other he handed her a sealed letter bearing the family crest. Several hours later, in the light of the candles burning in a consecrated chapel, Aurelia, sitting beside her mother's coffin, opened the letter with a shaking hand and read.

That same night General Heredia's pretty wife, Juana, alone in her boudoir, was leaning back against the cushions on a divan. Her carefree pose was in stark contrast to the expression on her face, which showed evidence of a violent internal struggle. With one hand she fiddled distractedly with the curls in her hair and in the other she held a closed book on which she rested her pretty head as if, tired of searching for something in its pages, she had turned instead to her lively imagination to find it. A discreet hand gently knocked on the glass door, which was lined with pink taffeta.

"Who's there?" asked Juana, putting on a sleepy voice and closing her eyes.

"A veiled woman wishes to speak with your ladyship," said a servant through the half-open door. When she heard the secret word, Juana's pretty eyes opened wide in all their magnificent splendour. A huge wave of curiosity washed away the concerns that had been troubling her and, shaking off her languor and rising softly to her feet, she exclaimed with all the excitement of a small child, "A veiled woman! Tell her to come straight in!"

And, lacking the patience to wait, she ran to meet the stranger. But as she crossed the threshold a woman in mourning, shrouded in a heavy veil, flung herself into her arms and pushed her back. She closed the door behind her and, turning to Juana, she took off her veil.

"Aura! What are you doing here, when your mother's corpse is still laid out in the house in mourning? My angel, what new misfortune has befallen you? Tell me!"

Aurelia, pale and trembling, gave a quick glance around the room and, going up to Heredia's wife, held out a shaking hand and told her in a clipped voice, "I've come to ask you to keep your promise, Juana. Do you remember the day we first met?"

"Oh, how could I forget, my angel? My son was drowning in the deep pool at Montoya. Nobody dared to rescue the poor child and I was pulling out my hair, crying desperately and trying to break free from the arms of those who were holding me back from jumping into that terrible whirlpool after him.

Then you arrived and, jumping out of your carriage as quick as a flash, all dressed in muslin and garlanded with flowers, you bravely hurled yourself into the water and wrenched him from a certain death. I threw myself at your feet and, clutching your knees, I told you, 'If you or any of your loved ones should need my life, you only have to ask me and I shall give it to you with pleasure.'"

"And so, a life for life. I saved your son; now in his name you must save Fernando de Castro."

"The Bolivian conspirator!" Juana exclaimed, fixing the young woman in a reproachful stare. "Perhaps you are not aware that the revolutionary movement he was leading has sworn to see both our husbands dead?"

"I know that and yet I come to say to you, honour your word!"

Juana's eyes shone with a glint of mischievous irony.

"Ah!" she said, "I guessed it that night when you first set eyes on that man: you're in love with him!"

Aurelia looked her friend straight in the eye and replied in a firm voice, "Yes, I love him."

"You're in love with him and you're married to Aguilar! Poor woman!"

"I love him," the young woman repeated, "I love him. But look at my forehead. Do you notice any hint of shame?"

"No, it's glowing as bright as an archangel's halo," Juana exclaimed, kissing her friend's clear forehead effusively.

"Yes, trust in the honest nature of the feelings which brought me here to you. But, in the name of heaven, let's not waste any time! Each hour that passes the fatal moment comes nearer. The court martial has passed sentence, Heredia has confirmed it and Aguilar is charged with carrying it out."

"Court martial! Heredia! Aguilar!" Juana exclaimed despondently. "All of them impervious to my powers of seduction! My God! What can I do to countermand their decisions?"

"I don't know. All I know is that you made me a promise and you must keep it."

"I'll keep it even at the cost of my own life, for the angel who rescued my son."

"Well, just remember what I expect." And Aurelia folded her arms and stood there, silent and motionless.

"By all the demons in Hell!" Juana murmured, changing her tone and allowing herself to be swept along by the friendly ebullience which never abandoned her, even in her most difficult moments. "All you demons, who constantly tempt me to be jealous, to hate, to harbour vengeful desires, inspire me for once to do something good! For example, tell me how to fulfil the vow, as demanded by this pretty young woman, to achieve such a tremendous thing. Heredia's will is all powerful and who am I to Heredia? If only I were Fausta! Now, that would be something else."

And a flash of anger shone in Juana's dark eyes.

"Mistress," said a woman's voice from the other side of the door.

"Rafa," shouted Juana, going out to meet the newcomer.

Rafa came in. She was one of those beautiful mulatta women from Córdoba, with a slender figure and languid blue eyes, whose golden curls seemed to have permanently captured the Argentine sun.

"You're so late today, Rafa. I've been waiting for you so impatiently! And yet my heart trembles at the thought of the new tribulations you bring me each day. Today, for example, I can see in your eyes yet another sorrow to add to the ones that have long since been destroying my heart.

But speak and tell me everything, I'm simply dying to hear!"

XII   THE SPY

Juana was pale and there was a sorrowful anxiety in her eyes, like a person torn between hope and fear. The mulatta woman sitting at her feet eyed Aurelia, who had covered her face with the veil again, with suspicion. Then she said, "May I speak?"

"Speak!" Heredia's wife said, "Tell me about that woman, who occupies my thoughts all day and my worst dreams all night. Is Alejandro with her?"

"Last night they both departed for Castañares, where tomorrow she will give a banquet for her followers. But I'm starting at the end . . . Listen, my mistress," the mulatta continued in a low voice, "even if it shall cause you great sorrow."

"When a heart's full of anger, don't be concerned about sorrow. Speak."

"Yesterday she was in her boudoir, lying back on a pile of burgundy velvet cushions. Naturally, she was dressed all in white, in a transparent muslin dressing gown, low cut with hanging sleeves which left her arms, breasts and shoulders bare. She was holding an album which she was leafing through, humming a piece from an opera. I was tidying up her room next door and watching her from behind the curtains hung across the door. The General came in and sat on a stool at her feet.

'What?' she said to him. 'So you just come in, like a Sultan in his lover's house, without bothering to ask how she is?'

'How can I help myself? She's always so beautiful and seductive,' he replied, stroking her long curly hair, so typical of the women from her native town of Santiago del Estero."

Juana ran her hand nervously through her own black hair.

Rafa continued. "Oh, it pains me to hurt my mistress, but she has ordered me to tell her!"

"Speak!"

"The General brought those curls to his lips. 'Sacrilege!' she cried, gathering up her hair with feigned annoyance. 'Didn't you know that poets have worshipped her and dedicated hymns in her honour?'

'Let them sing!' he replied, laughing. 'Let them sing to the object of my devotion!' And he started leafing through the album. 'Nonetheless,' he added, 'I envy them their divine talent for expressing the exuberance of the soul so melodiously.'

'What I wouldn't give to see the name of Alejandro Heredia, beneath a thought of yours, in that book!'

'Well,' said the General, stretching out and picking up a pen from a nearby writing table. 'Genius has filled this book with eulogies; but the hand of Power needs only one line at the bottom of this page to create a talisman that will make you absolute sovereign of the city of Tucumán, as far as the banks of the Tumusla river.' And the General signed his name at the bottom of a blank page."

Juana stamped her pretty foot on the floor and her eyes blazed with a sinister glow behind her black eyelashes.

Rafa continued. "Fausta examined that signature scornfully. 'Ah!' she said, shaking her head sadly. 'What can I do with this double-edged sword you've placed in my hands? Even though I'm surrounded by enemies, I have no wish to meet evil with evil. I suffer for you: that is consolation enough for me!'

'Who could set eyes on you or listen to you speak and not fall at your feet!' the General cried, getting down on one knee and kissing the toe of her white satin shoe which peeped out beneath her skirt."

"Enough", Heredia's wife exclaimed in a quavering voice. "Rafa, I need that book. Go and fetch it for me and return here immediately. What are you waiting for? Go!"

"There's still more, my mistress."

"Have you been listening, oh heart of mine? Well, steel yourself and listen on!"

"Fausta smiled tenderly at the General, then pulled a face and sighed. 'But I confess to you, my generous Alejandro (oh, what a lovely name you have, Alejandro)–what was I going to say?–Oh yes–that among those enemies there is one whom I am head over heels in love with . . .'

The General's face flushed red with anger and he glared at Fausta ferociously. She leant back on his shoulder, looked up at him with fawning eyes and said in a low voice, 'Do you know who he is, Alejandro? You'll never guess who this rival is, and perhaps you won't let me have him, either. It's a racing certainty that you know him well. They say that he runs like the wind. Oh, how I would love for him to take me for a single run with you on your bay horse, beyond the limits of this world, to unknown places created by fantasy in golden dreams, the house of free and eternal love . . . Oh, here I am again, Alejandro, as always when I'm at your side, in the regions of the sublime. I'm scared of the steep descent down to the stables where the object of my desire resides.'

'He's yours,' the General told her."

"Tenebroso," cried Juana before the mulatta could repeat her husband's final words. "Tenebroso, my speedy mount, the handsome colt that I stole, seduced by his beauty, from the herd of wild horses!"

"He's been in Fausta's stables for the past four hours."

"Ah," exclaimed Juana in a gloomy voice. "And people say that vengeance is wrong, even when the affront is so grave! I'll kill that woman!"

"Juana, what are you saying?" murmured Aurelia, getting up from the divan, trembling.

"Aura, oh, forgive me my darling. I'd forgotten you were there!" But as she spoke, Juana's face suddenly lit up with a sinister look of delight and, turning to the mulatta, she said, "Rafa, do you love me?"

"Do I love her, my mistress asks me!" the mulatta cried, looking at Juana adoringly. "You might as well ask if the earth loves the sun, or if the angels love God. Oh, who was it who wrenched me away from the savage cruelty of the master who condemned me to suffer a daily torment; from the arms of a tyrant and an executioner's whip? Oh mistress," the mulatta continued, throwing herself at Juana's feet and looking up at her with her beautiful eyes, radiant with zeal, "I'm indebted to you body and soul, and my most ardent desire is to find the occasion to thank you by offering some great sacrifice. My mistress wanted me to spy on Fausta Belmonte, and I became her favourite maid in order to get close to her, to be able to relate her most intimate desires, the beating of her heart, and I closed my soul to her fond caresses and instead abhorred her with as much hatred as my mistress has for her. I know that it's wrong, that it's a crime. So much the better! I'll have done something in your service. And if one day my mistress should say to me, 'Rafa, you have lived long enough, it's time to die,' Rafa would die happily at your feet."

XIII   SELF-DENIAL

"Well then, Rafa, I need to begin a campaign of ruthless, relentless vengeance against that woman, on a daily, hourly basis, and throw back in her face the chalice of pain and humiliation she's forced me to sup for so long."

"Tell me what you want me to do, mistress," Rafa replied eagerly. "What do you want of your slave? Here's my dagger; just say the word and I'll stick it through your enemy's heart."

"No, I wouldn't be avenged by her death. She would die being loved! That would be an apotheosis! No, I want her to weep as I've wept; I want her to suffer desperate, sleepless nights, as I've done; I want anger to wither her heart and destroy her beauty as it has destroyed mine. I'll start today, and first of all I order you to bring me that album right now, and to take Tenebroso out of her stables and leave him somewhere remote, saddled up and ready for a rider. And after that, come back here."

The mulatta stood up and went on her way.

Aurelia turned towards Juana without saying a word and showed her the time. It was ten o'clock.

"One moment longer, my beauty," Juana said. "One moment longer and you shall see me fulfil my promise. And I shall see the start of my vengeance!" she added in a dull voice.

Rafa was back before long, bringing a book which she placed in Juana's impatient hands. It was one of those magnificent Keepsake books,[22] with fabulous English engravings. She opened it and ran her shaking fingers over its golden pages with a feverish anxiety, carelessly defacing the artistic treasures and talent that graced them.

"Arcadia!" she suddenly cried out, looking at a beautiful illustration representing a pastoral scene with a pretty cottage. "Arcadia! Our estate! Infamy! Does he dare to place my house, his wife's home, my ancestral inheritance, among his strumpet's shameful trophies! Here she is," Juana continued, looking maliciously at the portrait of a beautiful woman, "Here she is. Her impudent eyes and her cynical smile betray her true self."

Beneath this portrait there were some magnificent lines by the poet Ascasubi,[23] with this sentence by George Sand[24] describing a woman, as an epigraph: *'As splendid as the sea, as fierce as a storm'*.

"And yet," Juana continued, examining the pretty composition with a grave look in her eyes, "Genius, the most sublime thing on earth after virtue, comes eagerly to grovel before these clay idols, unafraid to muddy its white wings!" And she turned the page scornfully.

Overleaf was the blank page with a signature that Juana

read without blinking, silent and motionless, her lips twisted into a withering smile.

"Now you'll see," the wicked brunette cried with bitter sarcasm, shaking her head. "I'll make you regret this signature. With it you delivered your honour and even your wife's life up to the mercy of an adventuress." And, tearing out the page, she sat at her desk and wrote two lines on it with her left hand.

"Here is the life you asked me for, dear Aura," she said, holding out the sheet of paper to Aurelia, who took it hurriedly. "Here it is, but I in turn will impose a condition on you."

"What is it? Tell me quickly!"

"Do you accept it?"

"Even if it should cost me my life."

"Well then, listen carefully."

As she spoke, Juana took a dress made from transparent white muslin out of her wardrobe, together with a veil and a hooded cape, both also white. Ever so gently, she removed Aurelia's lugubrious clothes and dressed her in the magnificent garments.

"Juana, what you ask of me is a profanity. This worldly outfit prevents my soul from mourning!"

"I beg it of you, dear Aura. And also I ask that when you present this order to the commander of the guards holding the prisoner, you cover your face like this." And Juana lowered the veil over her friend's face.

"I understand," Aurelia murmured, and she left quickly along streets that were deserted at such a quiet hour. "Poor Juana. Envy has darkened your beautiful, noble soul. Today you want to avenge yourself and tomorrow you'll bitterly regret having done so. No, it will not be like that, no. I'll take it all upon myself and I'll spare your pretty heart, already so broken, from feeling any remorse."

And, as Juana paced up and down her room feverishly, but smiling at the prospect of a vengeance soon to be realised, which she savoured in advance with the bitter sensuousness of hatred, the spirited and determined young woman went on her way to carry out her dangerous mission. A bright light shone in her soul and dissipated the doubts that had tormented her, and now she walked with a firm step, guided by her conscience. And so she walked up the streets that climbed gently towards the San Bernardo barracks, at the foot of the hill which bore the same name.

The barracks, converted from an old monastery, rose before her, imposing and silent, presenting a dark mass against the blue sky. From time to time, the sharp sound of the alarm being raised by the sentries from their stations in the towers and attics of the old building could be heard, like the screeching of some nocturnal bird.

Aurelia knocked resolutely at the main door of the barracks and asked to speak to the commander of the guard. Such was the importance of his orders that the officer on the other side of the door was standing to attention with his hand on his sword. He gave orders for the door to be opened. Under the moonlight, in the doorway, his eyes met the elegant figure of a woman dressed all in white, her face hidden under the folds of her veil. She took a step towards him and held out a document.

The officer looked her over quickly and took the document, murmuring, "That eccentric attire. That blend of courage and mystique. It must be her! She's come to serenade the General! I wouldn't put anything past that sorceress. It's her!"

But his train of thought quickly changed when he read the document in his hand. He rubbed his eyes and, not trusting the moonlight, he went to read it again under the lantern in the guardhouse. "No doubt about it," he said to himself. "The order is brief and unequivocal, like all General Heredia's orders. What a huge responsibility! And what if the General is feeling a bit . . . you know? He does like to have a joke, and on more than one occasion it's turned out to be the case . . . Madame, my Commanding Officer, Colonel Aguilar, is here, and . . ."

Aurelia shuddered.

". . . I'd like to speak with him before I hand over the prisoner."

"Impossible! The order that you've just read expressly forbids it. It forbids any discussion."

"Yes, that's true."

The officer disappeared into the arches of the cloister. He made a sign to the lieutenant of the guard, who put out the lantern and the barracks was left in dark shadows. Aurelia, shaking with anxiety, counted the minutes by her own heartbeat, but she didn't have to wait for long. Through the darkness she saw two men approaching arm in arm. One was the officer of the guard, the other was Fernando Castro. The officer placed the prisoner's hand into that of his liberator and accompanied them to the street. Then, leaning towards the prisoner's ear, he said to him in a voice that, despite his best efforts, betrayed a deep feeling of envy:

"You have to admit, Commander, that this is a drastic turn of the tables. My God! Out from behind those iron bars and into those beautiful arms, which have made the General lose his reason."

Those words, spoken with reference to the veiled woman, reminded Aurelia what the anxious expectation of the past hour had made her forget: the role that Juana wanted her to play in her act of revenge. Her face burned with the flush of shame and, approaching the officer who was just about to close the door, she pulled back the veil and showed him her face. Then immediately, covering her face again, she dragged the prisoner away with her, leaving the officer of the guard frozen in shock, crying out in terror: "The Colonel's wife!"

The prisoner fixed his gaze on his liberator and, suddenly stopping in his tracks, he said to her, "Celestial being, it's pointless trying to hide yourself. My heart guessed who you were the moment your hand touched mine."

"In heaven's name, Fernando, let's get away from this place. Delaying a minute longer could mean death for you and I came to snatch you away from the clutches of death at the risk of my own life and at the risk of my honour. Because I know, oh, you who I fell in love with when I first set eyes on you, I know what this invincible feeling that draws me to you is called."

"Love," cried the prisoner who, without realising it, was keeping pace with his guide's rapid steps, with his ears and his heart transfixed by those sweet words which swept to the core of his soul like waves of fire.

"Where are we?" Aurelia suddenly asked, stopping for lack of breath.

"On the lower slopes of the hill, beside the Yocci well,"

said the mulatta, who was following them at a distance.

Aurelia shuddered. The shadow of a terrible memory crossed her mind but she controlled her fear and looked all around. In a bend formed by a gully and a group of carob trees she saw the parapet and limestone pillars of one of those artesian wells, of which there are so many in the outskirts of the city. A magnificent horse, as black as ebony, was tied by its bridle to one of the well's pillars, and he impatiently pawed and stamped his hooves on the dry mud of this scantily grassed area.

"There is Tenebroso," Rafa added. "He's saddled up and ready for his rider, who has delayed too long already." And the mulatta went on her way.

XIV   THE SACRIFICE

"Everything you need in order to escape is here," said Aurelia, turning to her companion, who was staring at her ardently. "The perfect time, silence and a good horse. What are you waiting for? Go!"

"Flee? Flee without you? Separate, when we're united by love?"

"You poor fool!" cried Aurelia, stepping back, shocked by this revelation. "Don't say that word. It would be an act of sacrilege for us!"

"Ah," he replied, seizing the young woman's hand impetuously. "What name would you give to the feeling that I inspire in you, what name would you give to the sublime courage with which you have risked so much to save me? What name would you give to this sweet feeling, which is drowning my heart in a sea of delights? And that tender look you give me as you gaze into my eyes? What's that called? That's called love!"

He wrapped his arms around Aurelia. She pushed him away, horrified. A terrible thought suddenly occurred to her. In the innocent abandon of pure feeling, she herself had visualised the truth of the fatal error that had clouded the outlaw's soul and sustained him under the menace of death.

"Mother!" she murmured. "Forgive me. Another person is about to read your intimate secret, but I know that you will approve what I'm doing from up there in heaven. Oh mother, this is the only way to save him."

And, going up to Fernando, she gave him a tender, sorrowful look and, holding out a document she said to him, "So you want to know what this feeling is, that ties us together so closely, that's sweeter than love itself? Read, then, and kiss my forehead, let's kneel and pray together, then go!"

The young man took the document anxiously and unfolded it under the moonlight. But as he read it, his face turned pale, his eyes filled with terror and his hair stood on end.

"You're my sister!" he cried, in an outburst of pain and anger. "Oh mother!" he continued, hurling the document away from him, "I'll seek you out beyond the confines of this world, you cruel woman, slave to human pride, who wickedly abandoned the son born of your dishonour so that you could grace your tarnished brow with a halo of virtue; you who, separating brother from sister, were the reason that the sacred love that should have united us has become a criminal desire, a source of never-ending sorrow. I'll follow you down to the depths of hell itself, so that I can say, 'Damn you!' " And the outlaw jumped on the speedy horse and disappeared.

When she heard this terrible curse, Aurelia let out a cry and collapsed against one of the well's pillars in a faint. The strength was drained from her body and soul and a strange darkness flooded her brain, leaving her in a state that was neither unconscious nor awake. A hand touching her shoulder woke her suddenly from the detached state of mind into which she had fallen. Aguilar stood before her, pale, sombre and terrifying.

"You didn't fool me, you treacherous woman!" he cried in a dull voice, staring at his wife with a sinister glare. "I've known that you were in love with that Bolivian conspirator since that night he held you captive. And you denied it and your face flushed with virtuous indignation. And at the same time as you were besmirching your own honour as well as mine, you were preparing to help him escape the punishment that awaited him. What have you done with him? Speak! This is not your husband here before you, this is a judge who is going to pronounce your sentence and carry it out. What have you done with the conspirator? Speak!"

"I've saved him," Aurelia replied, "but my motives were not shameful, Aguilar, this was a pure, sacred act of affection, I swear to you."

"Prove it! Ah! I would sell my soul if I could only believe it!" And a tear ran down his pale cheek, and with a voice charged with sorrow and rage, he repeated, "Prove it!"

"And if I can only prove it by swearing an oath, will you believe me, Aguilar?"

"I knew you were lying!"

Suddenly, Aurelia let out a cry and picked up something and hid it in her bosom. It was the document that Fernando had thrown away, which was lying forgotten on the ground. Aguilar saw it.

"What's in that document? I need to see it."

"Never! It's my secret!"

Beside himself with anger, Aguilar leapt on his wife and, clasping her hands in one of his he shouted, "Will you give me that document?"

Aurelia, with a tremendous effort, freed her hands and shouted, "Aguilar, you can kill me if you like, but don't ask to read this document!"

Then there was a struggle: short, but terrible, between a strong person and a weaker one, between physical force and the sublime force of a powerful will. Aguilar tried in vain to snatch the document from Aurelia's tightly clenched fingers, as she held on to it with an iron grip.

"Give me that document," Aguilar repeated, blind with rage.

"No!"

"No?"

"No. A thousand times no."

Aurelia's voice was drowned in a dull groan. Aguilar's dagger was buried deep in her breast. The murderer seized the letter which was the price of his crime, and with the cold-bloodedness of a jealous rage sated, he unwound the red sash that he used to hold his weapons, tied a rock to his victim's neck and threw her into the well. And then, unfolding the document, which he clutched in a shaking hand, he held it up to the moonlight and read. Suddenly, the paleness of anger gave way to the paleness of horror. A red mist descended over his eyes, his heart stopped beating and his ice-cold tongue spluttered in a desperate voice, "He was her brother!"

Three days later, General Heredia, out walking with some ladies in the flower-laden wooded groves of San Bernardo, came across a pale, solemn man, his clothes in disarray, his head bare and his eyes staring into the distance.

"He's a madman," the ladies said, timidly hiding behind the General.

"No he isn't," said Heredia, recognising him. "He's the dishonoured husband of a shameless wife who, leaving her own mother's corpse unburied, ran off with the Bolivian conspirator."

Those words shook Aguilar out of the detached state of mind in which he was languishing. The vague thoughts that had been crashing around in his brain in heated waves suddenly took on a terrible clarity. The enormity of his crime and its fatal consequences came together in a single thought. Not only had he murdered his wife, but also by hiding his crime he had dishonoured her. A deep sense of remorse, an unspeakable pain invaded his soul and, running over to the General, he opened his mouth to confess his crime and exonerate Aurelia. But taking a second look into the depths of his conscience he found it so terrible that, for the first time in his life, he took fright and held his tongue.

From that day onwards his courage turned into savagery; his sorrow became an insatiable rage against the whole human race. In battle, in combat, and in the frequent military uprisings of the time Aguilar never gave any quarter; he killed pitilessly and gleefully, bathed in his victims' blood, avidly witnessing their death throes.

He was a cursed man. He wanted to forget, to bury the memory of his crime in an abyss of atrocities. Vain hope! Superimposed on the blood of the Bolivians and the rebel soldiers, he would always see someone else's blood railing against him; and rising above the combatants' cries and the screams of the dying he could always hear a dull moan, followed by the sound of a body plunging into water. Then, sinking his spurs into his horse's flanks, he would flee from wherever he happened to be, believing that he could flee from that bitter memory, and he would cross plains and forests and mountains, running, always running until his horse, exhausted, lifeless, collapsed beneath him. And the shepherds in those parts, seeing the sombre horseman passing through the mist at such a fantastic speed like a shooting star, would make the sign of cross and recite the most devout prayers, terrified, believing that he was the devil in the night.

XV   DEFEAT

One day Aguilar was at the head of his regiment, in the midst of an army in battle formation on the plain which extends to the Montenegro foothills. Opposite them, on the far side of the plain, stretched the lines of the Bolivian army.

Always thirsty for blood, Aguilar contained his impatience by scanning the ranks of his victims until the battle cry sounded. He did not have to wait long. Then the former brothers in arms who had fought together under the Nationalist flag of freedom, now separated by the fratricidal hatred of their political parties, one side bearing the black standard of the Argentine Confederation, the other the tricolour flag of the Peru-Bolivian Confederation, both of them symbols of degeneracy and ignominy, flew at each other like hungry tigers, turning that field into a sea of blood, littered with corpses.

At the fiercest centre of the combat, Aguilar saw a man with his sword unsheathed and dripping with blood who, like a flash of lightning, cut swathes through the Argentine battalions, leaving death and horror in his wake. There was something mysterious about this man's appearance that heightened the terror inspired by his fearlessness. His horse was as black as the night and his broad cape, which was also black, floated behind him in the wind, like the wings of doom.

Aguilar watched as his men shrank back when confronted with that formidable warrior. He flung himself upon him just as he was withdrawing his steaming sword from an enemy's chest, and ran him through with his own. The stranger turned on him like a tiger, but his strength suddenly failed him. He dropped his sword, stretched out his arms and his lifeless body slid from his horse, which carried on running and disappeared into the distance.

Aguilar, true to his barbarous custom, leaned over in his saddle to contemplate his victim. But when he looked at the face of the corpse, his eyes widened in horror and his hair stood on end. "Fernando de Castro!" he cried, motionless amid the clouds of smoke whirling around him. "Fernando de Castro!" he repeated. And a lugubrious voice rose up from the depths of his soul, screaming at him, "You murdered the sister! You killed the brother! You are cursed! Cursed! Cursed!"

Suddenly, a huge wave of fleeing men crashed into him and dragged him far away from the battlefield. Aguilar, blind with rage and wanting to kill and die, tried in vain to stop his soldiers, inflicting wounds on them mercilessly, but in spite of his efforts and those of the other leaders, the whole army broke ranks and the Argentines, for the first time ever, were routed by their enemies.

XVI   THE VOICE OF CONSCIENCE

A short while later one of the two armies in the southern region of Latin America was defeated in Ancasch and peace with Bolivia was restored. Aguilar, now confined, despite his character, to a life of inaction, couldn't bear to see the place where his crime had been committed and he fled Salta, taking refuge in the heart of the busy Metropolis of Buenos Aires.

Some years later he became chief of Rosas' secret police known as the Mazorca and shocked Buenos Aires with his brutality.[25] But, just as bloody combat could not sate him, neither could bloody murder, and the memories of the past always hovered over the horrors of the present day: fatal, inerasable, eternal. Desperate, in a bid to escape the delirium of madness which was starting to grip him, Aguilar became immersed in a world of vice. He divided his time between gambling, drinking and women; he revelled in orgies and outrageous behaviour, creating a whole court of slaves to licentiousness, which he ruled over with absolute power.

No drinker ever dared to fight with him; gamblers shook with fear when they saw the dice in his hands, because the outcome was never left to chance; and any woman he looked at just once would fall at his feet, forever smitten.

But, in the steamy world of orgies, as in the smoke and dust of battle, the pale shadow of Aurelia would always appear before his eyes, and in the midst of all the Bacchic songs there was always an echo of her final gasp.

So, seized by a strange frenzy, he lost himself in furious excess, broke and destroyed anything that came into his path, polished off spirits and opiates with no effect; seized the most beautiful of his dissolute playmates by the throat, squeezing her in his arms until he choked her and bloodying her lips with his manic kisses. And those women, worn down by vice, desperate for affection and fascinated by the mysterious power of this man whom they considered to be supernatural, gladly suffered and fought among themselves for the tortures that he deigned to inflict upon them.

XVII GOD'S JUDGEMENT

One riotous night, as he left one of these parties with a crowd of his drunken friends, Aguilar felt a cold hand on his shoulder. He turned round and saw beside him a woman dressed in white, her face hidden by a long veil.

"Which one are you, my beauty in disguise," he said to her gaily. "Margarita? Julia? Tránsito? Pepa?"

Silence. There was no reply from beneath the mysterious veil and all that could be heard were the discordant voices of the women he named screeching from the midst of the group, "What is it, darling Aguilar, why did you call me? Here I am, Aguilar."

"Well then," he continued, "whoever you are, I swear that you won't regret choosing me as your companion, and even if you come from the great beyond, I'll carry you in my arms if your little legs are tired of walking."

"Who could be so audacious as to speak about the other world at twelve o'clock midnight?" a pretty girl with olive skin called out, half excited and half frightened, from beneath her companion's cape.

"At twelve o'clock midnight, under the bitter *pampero* wind!" added another.

"That's Aguilar, who likes to flirt with his sword, as if it were a woman," said a captain of the halberdiers, laughing and cackling. "Gentlemen, hurrah! The King of the drinkers is finally drunk! Hurrah!"

Aguilar could hear his companions' happy voices in the distance as they continued their merry banter, while the mysterious lady attached her arm to his with the lightest of touches. They walked through the city, leaving the fields behind them and racing through the brambles, gradually getting faster and faster until, buffeted by a hurricane's lugubrious gusts, Aguilar could make out the plains, the forests and mountains flashing past at breakneck speed.

Suddenly, the white domes of a city appeared on the horizon, coming ever closer. And then they were there! Aguilar and his guide walked through the streets. In front of them was a bridge; a bridge he hadn't crossed for a long time past, a time full of bad memories. He wanted to stop, he wanted to go back, but it felt as if his arm was welded to the arm of the silent lady, who became more and more diaphanous as she dragged him along with her like a whirlwind, to the very edge of a well which he had never stopped seeing before his eyes, whether dreaming or awake.

And Aguilar was shocked to see how his companion's long clothes took on a vague, transparent form, now similar to a bride's white satin, now like a ray of moonlight on a misty lake; and the night's breeze folded back the foggy veil that covered her, allowing him to glimpse the pale face of a woman who smiled at him sadly, revealing a breast torn by a deep wound, and a voice like the howling wind brought these words to his ear:

"Here I am, husband of mine! Here I am, not glowing and pretty like I was at the altar, but pale and cold as when you first kissed me. Look, my wound is still bleeding, but you should be delighted with that, since you're so fond of blood. Oh, come closer! My hands are freezing, I'd like to warm them up on your chest. Come on! You've left me all alone in our marital bed for so long! I miss having you by my side, and I'd like to sleep in your arms for eternity! Come!"

Aguilar, speechless with terror, wanted to flee, but he was suddenly enveloped in the phantom's blue-white veil. A pair of lifeless lips smothered a scream of horror in his mouth and an icy arm clasped his body, which rolled forward and plummeted into the black depths of the well.

Notes

[1] Dreams and Realities, Buenos Aires, C. Casavalle, 1865.

[2] Circuito Pedestre, Material Orientivo y de Consulta para el Examen de Guías Idóneos, Gobierno de la Provincia de Salta, Lic. Carolina Mercado and www.cuartopodersalta.com.ar.

[3] Source: www.cuartopodersalta.com.ar.

[4] The Río Desaguadero runs from the north west of Argentina across some 1,500 km to join the Río Colorado south west of Buenos Aires. Its upper reaches are also known as the Río Bermejo or Río Vinchina; its lower reaches are also known as the Río Salado.

[5] Reference to the May Revolution of 1810, which took place in Buenos Aires from 18th May to 25th May, beginning the Argentine War of Independence.

[6] The Quebrada de León is close to the town of León, some 20 km NNW of Jujuy.

[7] The Battle of Vilcapugio (1813) was a famous defeat for the Republican forces led by General Manuel Belgrano by a Royalist army under Joaquín de la Pezuela, Viceroy of Peru.

[8] Psalm 43: Judge me, O God, and plead my cause against an ungodly nation: O deliver me from the deceitful and unjust man.

[9] Cierzo: a cold, dry wind that whips across the north of Argentina, named after a similar wind in north-west Spain.

[10] *Lasciate ogne speranza, voi ch'intrate (Abandon hope, all ye who enter here)*–the sign above the entrance to Hell in Dante's Inferno.

[11] A reference to the Gorriti family's own protracted exile, having fled from the dictator Manuel Rosas into exile in Bolivia, during the Argentina civil war.

[12] *Sarraceno* was a pejorative name for Royalist during the War of Independence. They were also known as *Godos* (Goths).

[13] The River Arias used to delineate the southernmost border of the city; before it was diverted, it followed the path now traced by Avenida San Martín.

[14] The Peru-Bolivian Confederation was established in 1836 as a new state comprising the Republic of North Peru, the Republic of South Peru and Bolivia. An Argentine invasion force was repelled in 1837 and the confederation was dissolved two years later, with Peru and Bolivia reverting to independent states.

[15] A reference to Juan Manuel de Rosas, elected as Governor of Buenos Aires in 1829 and de facto dictator of the Argentine Confederation. He was ousted in 1852 and fled to England, where he lived in exile until his death in 1877.

[16] La Quiaca is on the present-day border between Argentina and Bolivia, about 290 km north of Jujuy.

[17] Charles Maurice de Talleyrand-Périgort (1754-1838) was a French diplomat whose name became a byword for slippery diplomacy.

[18] Tilcara: a town some 55 km north of Jujuy; halfway between Salta and La Quiaca.

[19] Iruya: about 70 km north of Tilcara.

[20] Support for the *Federalista* party was indicated by a red rosette; during the Rosas dictatorship anyone not wearing one

was considered an enemy of the state and persecuted by the Mazorca.

[21] Joaquín de la Pezuela (1761-1830) was Viceroy of Peru and commander of the Royalist troops during the Argentine War of Independence. After defeating General Belgrano at the Battle of Vilcapugio in 1813, the following year he went on to occupy Jujuy and Salta. He was forced back by the guerilla tactics deployed by General Martín Miguel de Güemes' gaucho army.

[22] The Keepsake was a literary anthology of romantic narrative, poetry and essays, published in London from 1827 to 1856. It was bound in scarlet silk and aimed at a young female readership.

[23] Hilario Ascasubi (1807-1875). Argentine poet, politician and diplomat. He published four volumes of poetry. Following the civil war, he spent much of his life in exile.

[24] George Sand was the pen name used by Amantine Lucile Aurore Dupin (1804-1876), a French romantic novelist and a socialist. She was a feminist *avant la lettre*, preferring to dress in men's clothes and smoking large cigars in public. She married at an early age but separated from her husband and famously embarked on a series of romantic affairs. One of her lovers was Frédéric Chopin. More importantly, she wrote nearly 60 novels and more than a dozen plays.

[25] The *Mazorca* was a secret police force set up by the *Sociedad Popular Restauradora* in 1840 and used by Juan Manuel de Rosas to identify and summarily execute any opponents to his regime. It was disbanded in 1846.

Also available from The Clapton Press:

SPANISH PORTRAIT by Elizabeth Lake

ISBN 978-1-9996543-2-0

Set principally in San Sebastián and Madrid between 1934 and 1936, this brutally honest, semi-autobiographical novel portrays a frantic love affair against the backdrop of confusion and apprehension that characterised the *bienio negro*, as Spain drifted inexorably towards civil war. It was described by Elizabeth Bowen as "A remarkable first novel [revealing] a remorseless interest in emotional truth".

Elizabeth Lake was the pen name adopted by Inez Pearn, a girl from a working-class background who won a scholarship to Oxford in the early 1930s and later joined the campaign for Britain to provide support for the Spanish Republic. She went on to produce five novels.

Along the way she was briefly married to Stephen Spender and subsequently, more enduringly, to the poet and sociologist Charles Madge.

This edition of Spanish Portrait includes an afterword by her daughter, Vicky Randall.

Also available from The Clapton Press:

BOADILLA by Esmond Romilly

ISBN 978-1-9996543-0-7

Esmond Romilly (1918-1941) was Winston Churchill's nephew and rumoured to be his illegitimate son. Already notorious as a teenage runaway from Wellington College, Romilly was among the first British volunteers to join the International Brigades in Spain, cycling across France to fight on the side of the Spanish Republic against Franco's insurrection. He saw intensive front line action in defence of Madrid, culminating in the battle of Boadilla del Monte in December 1936.

Written on his honeymoon in France after eloping with Jessica Mitford in early 1937, this is his personal account of those events, in which many fellow comrades lost their lives. As well as a highly readable and moving memoir, it has served as a primary historical source for many leading scholars writing about the Spanish Civil War, including Paul Preston, Hugh Thomas and Anthony Beevor.

This annotated edition includes an introduction, together with an appendix with three poems written in Spain by the poet John Cornford, who died fighting for the Republic.

Also available from The Clapton Press:

SOME STILL LIVE
by F. G. Tinker Jr

ISBN 978-1-9996543-8-2

Frank G. Tinker was a freelance US pilot who signed up with the Republican forces in Spain because he didn't like Mussolini. He was also attracted by the prospect of adventure and a generous pay cheque. Once over in Spain he took on the bombers and fighter pilots lent to the Fascist rebels by Hitler and Mussolini, who used the Spanish Civil War as a practice ground for the mass bombing of civilian populations. Tinker chalked up the largest number of acknowledged enemy kills, shooting down a total of 8 Junkers, Fiats and Messerschmitts. When he returned to the US he was unable to rejoin the Armed Forces and, depressed by Franco's victory, he was found in a hotel room in June 1939 with an empty bottle of whisky and a bullet in his head. This is his account of his experiences in Spain.

Also available from The Clapton Press:

MY HOUSE IN MÁLAGA
by Sir Peter Chalmers Mitchell

ISBN 978-1-9996543-5-1

In 1934 Sir Peter Chalmers Mitchell retired at the age of 70 from a distinguished career as Secretary of the Zoological Society of London. During his tenure he had been the driving force behind the creation of the Whipsnade Zoo, which opened in 1931.

He moved to Málaga "for what I expected to be a peaceful old age" and spent his time writing his memoirs and translating novels by Ramón J. Sender. Then came the rebellion of 1936. While most other British residents fled to Gibraltar, Sir Peter was one of the few to stay in order to protect his house and garden, and his servants.

Although an open sympathiser with the Anarchist cause, he provided a safe haven to the wife and five daughters of Tomás Bolín, members of a notorious right wing family, eventually helping them escape across the border.

He later offered shelter to Arthur Koestler. When the Italian forces sent by Mussolini to support the rebellion took Málaga, they were both arrested by Tomás Bolín's nephew, Luis, who was Franco's chief propagandist and who had vowed that if he ever laid his hands on Koestler he would "shoot him like a dog".

This is his memoir of that period, first published in 1937.